LOTANDO UREY

THE TORTURE CHAMBER

Tatenda Charles Munyuki

LOTANDO UREY

THE TORTURE CHAMBER

Tatenda Charles Munyuki

Darling Kind Publishing

LOTANDO UREY: The Torture Chamber

First published in Zimbabwe in 2014
Darling Kind Publishing
an imprint of Tatenda Charles Munyuki Publishing

ISBN   978 0 7974 6163 5

Printed and bound by Darling Kind Publishing, Harare, Zimbabwe.
darlingkindp@live.com

facebook.com/tatendacmunyuki

www.tcmpublishingzim.com

..........Eloi, eloi, lama sabachtani?

Matthew 27:46

CHAPTER ONE

Coincidental Harlot

All she had wanted to have was a drink and some fun on her birthday with her friends. *Was that too much to ask for?* She thought staring down.

She figured herself to be subconscious, but the urine's stench was killing her. Squeaky, frightened and drunk feminine voices feasted her ears. Her eyes were so sore that she tried not to think, but it wasn't easy.

My life, as usual, is so disappointing, she thought.

With the measure of darkness, it was about ten in the evening. Spending her twenty-first birthday's night in jail with an assembly of whores wasn't what she had had in mind.

It had all began when she had accompanied her friends to a new shopping mall in town around three o'clock in the afternoon. They had had a couple of drinks, not celebrating anything of course, as her friends didn't know when she was born. The group of friends consisted of Debra – her roomie at college – and Fadzai.

After having some *free* red wine, Debra had received a call from her sister requesting a brief meeting. Debra's sister lived at an apartment close to one of the worst slums in Mutare, a very controversial place found in the city. It was called *The Paradise of Pleasure, the PP*. Accompanying Debra, Fadzai had suddenly had this nearly all craziest, but cool at the time idea. Time was flying and they needed to be back at the college before six. Near the flat was a shortcut that could have saved them some valuable time – at least that's what Fadzai had suggested.

It was a dark nook street-like path and only *love sellers* were seen lingering. They hadn't seen any harm by just passing by. At that time of the day, especially with it being a Friday, the *lovers' path* was always loaded with *merchandisers*. The three ladies had made it perfectly clear that they were just passing through not wanting to cause any upset by unfortunately being mistaken as *location poachers*. Like always, coincidences took hell.

At that moment, everyone at *lovers' path* had been arrested by a team of daring cops. That was how she and her dear friends had ended up at the Police Station designated as cunning prostitutes.

She looked up and saw her friends having an argument about something of getting into trouble with their parents.

'Please don't worry, Tamara will get us out of this in a sec,' Debra said.

Fadzai sulked and placed her hands on her hips. 'What can your sister possibly do to get us out of this mess? Oh my God, my parents are going to kill me.'

The *birthday girl* glanced in a corner and saw a real prostitute playing with an empty toilet tin. *Arghhh, so disgusting.*

'Tami happens to be a lawyer,' Debra whispered.

'What!' Fadzai mouthed. 'What are you talking about, Deb? She is a secretary, for crying out loud.'

'She is a lawyer by profession. Please don't argue with me, Fadzi, I know what I'm talking about.'

A lawyer? Maybe that's why she is so smart and all, but why live in a flat, especially one close to lovers' path? The birthday girl thought confused.

'She said she'll be here just now when I talked to her on the officer's phone,' Debra asserted.

Of all days, she had been arrested on her birthday for doing nothing and learned that her roommate's sister was a lawyer *posing* as a secretary. Life couldn't get odder. *What could be next?* Only the heavens knew.

CHAPTER TWO

Phi Flux

She didn't actually know how the journalist got them, but they were now infamous. They had appeared on *The Chronicle's* front page, *The Herald's* fourth page, *Daily News'* sixth page and *H-Metro's* first page – not to mention many Facebook pages. *Prostitutes Nabbed*. Although the campus wasn't usually packed with students the following week, they were on top of the attraction list.

Making matters worse, her uncle had called her to give her a, *"what the fuck is up?"* To save herself from a rather harsh endless phone call, she had referred him to Tamara the *lawyer* and hung up. It wasn't that she hated him, but he loved her and she didn't.

Her name was Lotando Urey. Age, she would say she was conceived rather too early or was very unlucky to have been conceived at all. Brunette and extremely light in complexion, some claimed she was almost albino. Although she wasn't really familiar with what six-foot meant or anything, everyone said she was tall enough to be a model. If she were classified as beautiful, that would have been insincere. Furious teenage years of hormones had shaped her body into more than a representable one. She was *simply* gorgeous in mysterious ways. She wasn't proud of it, neither did she envy it. She just lived with what her Mama had given her.

If people talked about what her race could be, it would be an inconclusive debate – a racial argument of hot conspiracy. Even she didn't know what she really was. *Lot*, as her buddies called her, was half-Caucasian, half-Indian, half-African, half-Colombian, half-European, pretty much half anything that comes to mind with extreme light pigmentation and looking a bit Latino in it. Personally, she thought she was half of nothing. Lotando saw her life as a commutation; the process where the apparent reversal in the direction of current flows is achieved.

Born on the 1ˢᵗ of November, she would rather claim that she was born a month and twenty-four days early. She could have shared her birthday with Jesus, not that she was a Christian in practice anyway. She had tried hard, but religion wasn't her kind of thing. She tried to live her life as simple as she could, but the harder she always tried the more complex it became.

Lotando was born the only child to a lawyer who was openly and discreetly rumoured to be a controversial socialite – she had grown up hating the idea of lawyers. Lately, she guessed it to be in the family. Christine Urey had never really had time for her daughter, and when she had passed away, her daughter had felt no loss at all. Lot was raised by many nannies and it was sad that she practically remembered none. If her memory served her well, it was only a few times each month that she had seen her mama. The people whom she had often seen were her grandparents.

Her academic life had been good, but she had lacked the essential things in life like a mother's love. She was sent to a boarding school where her life had changed into a revolting one. She had been lucky though to be sent to a girls' mission school called Monte Carron, but was unfortunate enough to discover what happened at these schools.

The use of unripe bananas as artificial partners, lesbianism, gossip and a whole lot of other things one couldn't clearly fathom had made her feel like a total idiot. This had left her with only three friends at a school of more than three hundred and fifty pupils. Lotando had to spend six measly years at school trying to find herself, but they had ended far too quickly before she had even started. Getting twelve points for her Advanced Levels after studying very hard had only made her feel insecure. In her opinion, her life seemed like one big joke.

BSc (Honours) in Electrical and Computer Engineering was what she was doing – not by choice, but destiny.

Being a third year at Mutare University, *MU*, only complicated matters for her. There was just so much to do, so much to think about and not to think of.

Oh girl, I wish I was dead. She could have chosen Law or Medicine, but then she didn't have the points and the subjects. She loved computers, no offence, but she hated the courses they were currently doing. At MU, they actually concentrated more on theories rather than on practical approaches. As her sixth form Mathematics teacher used to say, *"If it gives you bother, don't bother, do another"*. But then if life could be as darling as that she thought she would have been a Lawyer by now.

Lotando's odd hate-love passion for Law, she figured, was probably because she was more like her mother was than she would have liked to believe. Maybe it was because she was curious of who her mother had really been in life. She estimated that she would probably die without even knowing who she really was. With time, she had learned not to care. She was just waiting for that day when *Lot* would turn into a pillar of salt and be like his wife, being no more, but a name for people to read about.

She didn't want to talk about her life because she saw herself ending up crying, blaming many people, or perhaps thinking of killing someone. It wasn't that ugly a life, but it wasn't that nice also. It was just one of those things one wishes had never occurred. She just wished that Lotando Urey wasn't born.

CHAPTER THREE

Resistance

Christine Urey had passed away from ovarian cancer when Lotando was thirteen. Only then had *some* of the truth been presented to her. Lotando's mother had had her titled with her maiden name, thus her father was never known.

Her uncle, Lloyd Urey – her mother's sibling of a family of two children – had won a very convincing bid to acquire Lot into his custody from her grandparents. He had almost had a fistfight with Grandpa Urey on that issue, but it had turned out that Lloyd was a very persuasive man. Her uncle had claimed that he owed everything to Lot's mother regarding to have evaded many unproven criminal charges due to Christine's prior vast influence as a reputable lawyer.

Lot's uncle was an individual one could call a *fraud expert*. During her holidays when she returned home for school holidays, Lotando had picked up many tricks and traits about dealing using the persuasive language. Almost everyone in the business cycle knew Lloyd Urey. His advice was gold to anyone who desired swift success. Uncle Lloyd was a rich bugger, although he never showed it. His half-balding head and plummeting belly made him look like an ordinary citizen. He was usually mistaken for a school's headmaster.

Her uncle had two kids, a seventeen-year-old boy, Winster, and a twenty-three-year-old lady, Yana, who learned at MU like her. These two resembled their mother because they looked nothing like their father. Winster was practically a shy boy who possessed his father's enchanting talents. Although he was relatively silent, when he spoke, everything he said was intellectual. He always left you wondering.

Yana, the envied cousin sister, was a medical student in her fifth and final year at *MSM, Mutare School of Medicine,* which was under MU. For this, Lot envied her the most. She was practically everything Lot wanted to be, with the exception of being somewhat freaky. Some people often stated that they looked like each other in certain ways, mostly their eyes. Since they were after all cousins, Lot didn't think much of it. For some undefined reason, Lot liked Yana in a way, and loved young Win. Perhaps it was because they were the only family she had.

Spending a Sunday's afternoon sitting at MU's rear recreational park was pleasant, especially with your friends. The ladies inhaled the nice November breeze as it kissed their cheeks and licked their eyes. Debra and Nyaradzo were sharing an iPad. Fadzai and Celestine were flipping over various fashion magazines and annoyingly screeching like a pair of hanging roosters at something they considered nice.

'You know, I don't actually know if I'll ever be so exposed.'

Lotando looked up from her daydream. Yana was sitting at her opposite, reclining on the lawn, grimacing. She looked so captivating in the November's glowing sunshine. She was flipping over a book, which surely wasn't Medicine. Lotando gasped because it was rather bizarre to see someone so old, so learned and who was going to be a fully-fledged doctor in a few months reading a novel, a *Nancy Drew* for that matter.

'Exposed?' Lot asked, partly confused.

'Yeah,' Yana smiled under the book.

Lot didn't actually see it, but felt it and knew. 'Please don't,' Lot begged firmly.

'At least you are now known nationwide at only twenty-one,' Yana continued. She didn't care what Lot thought.

'Please!' Lot exclaimed furiously. 'Don't start on that, please.'

'Why not? Father was very amused.'

'Amused my ass,' Lot retorted, seethed by the fact that Yana was hiding behind the novel avoiding eye contact. 'Wouldn't you like to be a real whore and get yourself arrested? I think that will be very nice, wouldn't it?'

Yana slapped her book shut and started to laugh. This annoyed Lot even more. 'So how did you get yourself caught playing prostitute, Lot?'

That's when Lot realized that Yana didn't know the real story.

Could she have believed I am a prostitute? She shuddered inwardly. Lot related the story the most convincing way she could with the help of her friends. Yana laughed throughout the whole tale. Somehow, Lot was gratified when Yana saw it as funny.

Three down, Lot thought as she was still waiting to hear from Grandma Urey. For that reason, Lot had left her phone switched off at the hostels. *Thank heavens Grandpa isn't alive to see his granddaughter appear in the country's newspapers suspected to be a prostitute. That would have really caused his death*, she thought.

CHAPTER FOUR

WYSIWYG (What You See Is What You Get)

Lot tried to figure out whether she did or didn't love holidays. *At least they are different for a change*, she thought. *I am famous, infamous, as a whore.* No matter what came or gave, her once clean reputation from then stank. People in her neighbourhood loved you for your badness. They were never going to believe a true story. They enjoyed seeing you marred and she bet that some were even preparing a *Welcome Back Chisipite's Whore* banner.

Her uncle's house was situated in one of the most active parts of Chisipite, close to the shopping centre. It was difficult to avoid people there. And she bet all were dying to see Lotando Urey for once in her lifetime. *She had made the front page, hadn't she?*

During holidays, Lotando rarely got out that much and that was her policy through and through. Going out was basically Yana's hobby. As a result, the less people Lot knew, the less that knew her, and the better.

As Chisipite was a very flashy territory, most people who lived there were either filthy influential or wealthy. Kids had their own rides, played golf with their father's employees during the weekends and went to private schools. Her hood was a major habitat of Caucasians and Indians. Only two original Africans had managed to fit in. The weirdest part of it was that Lot liked their kids more than the other neighbours. Maybe it was because some of them were very down to earth and they minded their own business.

There was a good-looking young man called Tawanda who was Lot's age. Chenai was his attractive sister aged nineteen. They were the Muchemwa's children. Their father was an Economist and Mrs Muchemwa ran a fast food outlet somewhere in the CBD. The

Muchemwas were nice people – very amiable and sociable.

There were the Dotonas. They had two children – a twenty-four-year-old handsome man, a marvellous spender who really knew how to enjoy his parents' dough and assets. He was called Never. He was maybe a player or something like that, as Yana classified him, but he was so ever charming.

His little brother, Jack, was a sixteen-year-old fat spoiled brat. What amazed Lotando the most about this chubby boy was that he was also a very smart *balloon*. She sometimes thought that the more food he ingested the more brains he acquired.

Apart from these two cool neighbours, the others worth mentioning were the Hewstones. The Hewstones made sure they were seen as the most elite family in the hood. Uncle Lloyd always ranted about these people. They only wore imported clothes, ate large-sized pizzas for breakfast, exchanged automobiles like pants and spent their holidays in exotic locations like Hawaii. This only illustrated their children better. Their oldest Brenla was a year older than Lot and they didn't see eye-to-eye. She worked as an Executive at one of her father's companies. Lot never actually got the hang of what kind of companies Mr Hewstone owned, but he was a very successful man. Brenla drove a Bentley, something Yana and her father had debated about the previous year when Yana had demanded for one too. She was also rumoured to be intimate with a wealthy middle-aged man.

The reason Lot and Brenla didn't like each other was because of an *incident* Lot had tried to assist Yana do something very stupid when they were teenagers and got caught in the act. Brenla had broken up with her then-boyfriend because of the incident and she had despised the Urey girls ever since.

Her twenty-year-old brother Godfrey was currently at an expensive private college. Lot couldn't actually believe the schools he had actually gone to for seven years wasting his parents' money repeating his Levels. Godfrey cared less, his father cared less, and so did his mummy. It seemed like he was just waiting to inherit his father's heritage.

The last were two girls. One was in the fourth form whilst the other was in the second form at *Chisipite Senior School*. Lot didn't know much about them except that they had crushes for Win.

If Lot didn't think of the loner and sole habitant, Lot thought she would surely be *sinning*. There was Pastor Rosina. Whether he was Spanish, Italian, she didn't even know or give a damn, but he was so damn good-looking. Sometimes Lot thought that being in the late twenties and a cleric was a waste of space. Surely, he didn't get to live amongst these capitalists, so as to say, from stealing weekly offerings. His family had been rich and they had all died the most bizarre way one could think of. Rumours claimed that that's why he had turned Christian thus becoming a Pastor. He was a very peaceful man who cared less about anything, but old Hymns, Bible verses and Mass parish attendance. Lot had once ran into him and that had resulted in her attending a long church service. In fact, it had been Yana's fault. It was always Yana's fault if anything occurring to her included Father Rosina in it.

To stick to the facts, Lotando didn't want to be religious. She didn't think it was worth sacrificing. So many out there were Christians and so many Christians were living like hell.

CHAPTER FIVE

Multimedia Christmas

It was more like the *Superposition Theorem,* which stated that in any network made up of linear resistances and containing more than one source of emf – the resultant current flowing in any branch was the algebraic sum of the current that would flow in that branch if each source was considered separately.

Her particular network was made up of alphabetic excitement intertwined with current flowing into the branches of infinite boredom. Lotando used to enjoy Christmases not because of the presents and such, but for the desired relaxing time given as an acceptable excuse from studying.

That year's Christmas was more exciting however, basically because she was a star attraction. Everyone in her neighbourhood wanted to see the *front-page alleged whore.* As much as she could, Lot spent as much time locked up in her room. That was probably what she was doing at the current moment, two days to go from Christmas Eve.

Her small posh bedroom was found on a very lonely wing of Uncle Lloyd's colossal house. She had chosen it that way. Lot was reclining on her bed absorbing the music that was playing from her laptop at a distance away. Her sleepy gaze happened to be fixed at the door. Odd sounds were coming from it. The door suddenly gave an agonizing complaint. Yana appeared holding a pair of *she didn't know what* stainless steel sharp and crooked instruments. Her precious lock was broken. Before Lot could say anything, Yana pulled her up and thrust her onto her lazy feet.

'What the hell!' Lot blubbered still weak from imminent sleep.

'Quick – take a bath now,' Yana said. She walked to Lot's cabinets and produced her bathroom bag. She threw it at her. 'We are going somewhere.'

The bag punched Lotando on the face and she fell onto the bed only to be pulled back up. When Lot saw the tools in Yana's hands, she thought, *"Oh my God, she is going to murder me if I don't comply."* Yana's eyes looked it. Lotando lethargically picked up the bag and took a subconscious gaze at the supposed to be locked door. She saw bits of metal lying on the floor and wondered what her uncle was going to say.

'Hurry up, Lot. You can't spend the whole holiday locked up in this putrid room of yours,' Yana pushed her toward the door.

Lot staggered to the bathroom in fear of being pushed to it.

The destination for why her lock had been destroyed was unbelievably Father Rosina's house. The house looked more like a cottage, a very beautiful Goldilocks one indeed.

Yana dragged her into the Rosina's premises much to her astonishment weakening her even to protest. It was around four-thirty evening time. With the lights on, Lot guessed that Father Rosina was back from his church. Yana rang the doorbell with the zeal of a stator.

'Urey ladies,' the pastor greeted, opening the door wide for them, clearly noting them to enter. 'What a pleasant day, please come in.'

Yana was already in. Lot wished that her uncle had some spy cameras or something lurking around. He would have been really pissed to see daughter and niece unreservedly enter into a bachelor's house. Him being a pastor or not, he was still a man wasn't he? There was no telling what could have happened next when the door was closed. A threesome was always a possibility. Unwillingly, she followed Yana who had already placed herself in one of the sitting room's sofas.

'Father, have you considered our entry forms?' Yana shouted, before they were even seated.

The house's interior walls had a touch of a smooth marble colour oil paint and its furniture was probably dated way too old, ancient relics of the Rosinas. The sitting room looked like a soap opera's set although no fireplace existed as far as Lot saw.

'Manners, Ms Yana,' the pastor said in a soothing hoarse voice. 'How was your day, Ms Lotando?'

'Never sleepy,' Lot muttered. She received a cool smile and melted in awkwardness. She wasn't supposed to be there anyway. *What the hell are we doing here and what is it about this guy that makes him smile every time?*

'Do you have any news about our application forms?' Yana pursued, almost jittery. 'Did we pass the vetting process?'

Pastor Rosina shrugged. 'Of course, you passed. You are all approved as Anglicans and better, your uni is in the location's district. I'm surprised you were doubtful when you really wanted to go. The others were greatly confident, even your little one. Some faith you should acquire, Ms Urey.'

Yana cried out something of a delighted *"yes"*. Lot was confused, but she minded her own business.

'So you have approximately four months to prepare the stuff you are going to present, which must be easy for you,' Pastor Rosina cried out, disappearing in a direction of somewhere Lot figured out to be the kitchen.

He returned within a minute carrying two plastic *Coca Cola* bottles. He handed each to them. Lot thought of declining the polite offer, but that *smile* persuaded her with instant impulse. The drink was nice, mainly because of the chill that was in it. Lot drank in silence. Her cousin sister's flapping mouth couldn't just flap shut.

'We'll be ready,' Yana smiled at the pastor.

'Good. So your final most important exams will not be affected by the time you are going to be giving to this expedition then, Ms Urey?'

'Naaa!'

'Cool!' the pastor said, slipping into his favourite chair facing them. He picked up a porcelain cup filled with tea from a nearby stool and placed it on his lap. 'Is your father favourable to the idea?'

'I'm twenty-three and about to be a qualified physician, father doesn't dare interfere in my matters, or Lot's,' Yana said firmly.

Lotando was more confused by this, but thought nothing further of it.

'Okay, pardon me, Ms Urey,' the pastor sort of apologized. 'There will likely be mountain viewing, and sightseeing as in physical expeditions to those who like. You'll have to shape up physically during the next three months if you don't want to be misfits. The rest is a theory thing, your type of thing, I guess.'

Yana beamed and finished her drink in two swoops. 'You don't have to worry about us, we'll be ready.'

'Another thing,' the pastor raised his eyebrows, surprisingly looking at Lot. 'To prevent any lot and founds, and mostly encourage more human interaction, there will be no carrying of special electronic gadgets. Just thought you should know to prevent future disappointment. There will obviously be no electricity there to do with those.'

'We don't mind at all, as long as we will have some fun,' Yana grinned staring at Lot.

'I wouldn't expect you to worry,' the pastor said glancing at Lot. This made her feel awkward. 'I thought Ms Lotando should know. I think she'd have liked to carry one.'

'Carry what?' Lot finally asked.

'Something like a laptop or something like that,' he said sympathetically. 'You won't really mind not carrying anything like that, would you?'

Lot was jamming in her reasoning capacity. 'What do you mean carry my laptop, where?'

'Where you and Ms Yana will be going next year of course.'

Lot stared at Yana confused. Yana gave her an exceptionally guilty grin. Lot knew that something was up. She felt it all the way from her eyes to the back of the brain. 'Yana, can you please tell me what he is talking about,' she said jumping out of the seat. 'What the hell is going on, Pastor?'

'Oh, my Lord,' the pastor sighed. 'You signed something you didn't know or read?'

Lot spent that year's Christmas giving Yana her piece of mind. They fought the whole of the day, and for once in her life, Yana felt proud about it. They had talked more than before and Lot had actually spent less than seven hours in her room. The last days of the holiday turned out to be consumable as Lot discovered that in three months' time such days would really help if they were to go *there* as friends rather than foes. And yes she was going, all because of her meddling cousin sister.

CHAPTER SIX

Maximum Torque

It was mid-February the following year. The campus was full of excitement that semester. The controversy was long forgotten and Lot was genuinely glad. She was fresh in her third year's final semester and Yana was concluding a good five years at Mutare University. Lot felt rather sad that the next exams would be marking the end of Yana's existence at the campus and the outset of her new journey as a lone Urey. As usual, the lessons were stressful.

The month of March was a very difficult one considering that she had a mysterious April holiday to look forward to and their time was more required in the library and endless boring lectures. Time was flying as if it was eating their hairs off.

'Ms Urey!'

Lotando felt a sharp nudge on the shoulder and looked at the person beside her. His name was Munya – a charming friend of hers. He wore these cool spectacles that made him look intellectually sexy. He was the genius of their class. His eyes however had a current desperate nudge about them. He looked nervous.

'What's up?' Lot whispered. He shrugged and quickly looked away.

'Ms Urey?'

Lot knew immediately. There was no confusing that sharp phasing-voice. The class called her *Big Mama Profits*. She always talked about making profits from almost everything.

'Professor Gaza,' Lot responded, looking as guilty as she could at her sturdy form. It's not a sin, but her lecturer ate more than enough and enough to make her buy new suits almost every month. She was one stern fat old lady, and her attitude sometimes got on Lot's nerves. Her face looked like a wasp's, glaring at Lotando about something. Lot stared back. She knew a dozen of other students were staring at her and she had no idea why.

'The answer, Ms Urey,' Professor Gaza snapped at her.

Lot was sitting on the sixth bench, precisely in the middle of the lecture room. She felt small. 'I'm sorry, Professor, but I didn't get it,' she apologized – not humanly sorry.

This lecturer, she knew, envied her about something. Lot constantly assumed that it was all about her surname, having a profitable making uncle who had succeeded in numerous fraud dealings enough to make him live rich and clean in the present future. People as innocent as Professor Gaza had chosen to teach business and because fairness never won anybody wealth out there, these people weren't as successful and they envied those who were.

'Why, is my lesson boring you of the greater mind?' Professor Gaza sulked at her.

'No, Professor, I just didn't get the whole of your question.'

'Which part didn't you get, Miss Urey?'

Lotando cringed in her seat and looked at Munya. He was sweating big time – he wasn't going to help her out. She looked to her left. The woman sitting there purposefully avoided her glare as she looked directly at BMP. This was one of BMP's favourite things – catch, call out and humiliate students who didn't pay attention in her classes.

'Okay, I didn't get anything about your question, Professor. I'm sorry I wasn't paying attention.'

Professor Gaza blew a smoke of fury from her ears. 'So you don't think my lessons are worth paying attention at all, Miss Urey?'

'I am –' she tried.

'You know it all, don't you? What profits will you make then by selling computer technology if you don't want to hear anything I teach, little Miss?' Professor Gaza placed her hands onto her round waist and leaned over the lecturer' stand. 'You think offering illegal services will be more profitable?'

The crowd murmured.

This ignited Lotando's nerves. She tried to keep her temper's threshold below nuclear reaction.

'What kind of illegal services, Professor? I don't understand.' She perfectly understood, but she tested to see if BMP had the fat to articulate it openly in a class of more than fifty students.

'Something like lingering around dark nooks waiting for sick men who don't appreciate their wives in bed,' Professor Gaza dared with too much air.

The students were stunned. Lot was outraged in the process. She wanted to kill this fat bitch and donate her corpse to the *museum of obeses*.

'There is no such thing I think off,' Lot choked the words out.

'Somebody covered up your dirty indiscreet endeavours, hey? Wonder why someone so financially fortified would actually do such a filthy thing. Peer pressure, hey?'

Many were wondering if this was still a management lecture or some provoking lecture thrust upon Lotando and the others who weren't there. Lot bit her lip in order to remain as quiet as she could master. Her breath was under imprisonment.

Professor Gaza saw her eyes ever blazing, and enjoyed it. 'I thank the person who took and publicised that picture in the papers,' she continued in an apprehensive tone. 'Showing off that kind of thing lessens the rate of HIV in the country.'

'Tell me something I don't know already, you human-sized hippo,' Lotando couldn't just stop herself. She was now standing. 'What are you paid to do, provoke prostitutes or open your miserable fat throat to teach us about profits and how to sell our degrees when we are done here? I have had enough of you.'

Without thinking, Lot thrust her books into her backpack and kicked her way for the exit. The murmurs were too loud and she didn't give a hell about anything, but for some fresh air to escape. She didn't even take a glimpse at the must-be-stunned Professor BMP. Lot had never felt so better in her life and she knew it would cost her possible expulsion. For once, she didn't give a damn. Her life was damned already. It only needed to be wiped out permanently.

One of her Electronics' courses lecturer gave her many glares during the afternoon's lecture, but he didn't dare ask her or any of the class a question. His lesson was more pleasantly quiet.

Lotando had suddenly made it with the people at campus. She was now being called the *Hot Peppery Sophomore* for many were mistaking her for a second year student. She received many greetings that day and the next, from many people she had never seen before. Once more, she was a star attraction. Obviously, the news had travelled pretty fast around campus. Stories were however commingled with exaggeration. Some were claiming that she had landed into a physical fight with one of the professors and had beaten her to pulp. Some said she had verbalized the professor's family. It was all so mad.

There was one thing Lot was gladder about though. Yana was away on a week seminar at a rural hospital. At least when she returned to hear about her egos, Lot thought that she would have calmed down enough to avoid getting into a huge fight with her. She was definite that Yana was going to give her an elderly sister's tongue-lashing.

The one thing she wasn't happy about that Friday's afternoon – all lessons over to break for the weekend – was that the Dean had asked to see her in his office. Her feet were all shaky as she strolled towards his office.

The Dean's office was situated at an isolated infrastructure where only the staff members were found wandering. Lotando had never been there once in her three years at MU. It was very sad that the chance she got to visit it was possibly to be given some very bad news. She shivered and picked up her pace. She thought of Uncle Lloyd, Yana, Grandma and even Winster, her friends most of all. She was near tears.

CHAPTER SEVEN

Waveform Harmonics

Her options were fundamentally split into diversified mathematical proportions. She called it *Lot's Harmonic Analysis*.

Was she going to be expelled, or better — suspended? This wasn't high school where such disciplinary measures were altered into instantaneous punishments. At this level, everybody was regarded as a grown up, and nobody punished grownups the little one's way. It was either you were gone for some time or you were gone for good.

Lot entered the Dean's office to find a weathered woman sitting behind a very huge desk. The woman was of medium weight, with a mixture of grey and ashen hair. She was nearly as complexly built as Professor Gaza was, but her structure was less pumped. Thin-lensed specs puffed her eyes. She was one of those people Lot often saw less about thrice a semester. There was no telling if she was nice or haggard, but the expression she had at the moment registered nothing tangible as she was busy calculating something on a sheet of paper.

'Yes?' she whispered in a throaty voice without looking up.

Lot's feet were still shaky as she walked over the office's coffee brown carpet. 'Er —' she started.

'Wait!' the secretary raised a finger into the air without taking her eyes from the papers. She did a swift calculation and retraced her finger back to the paper. She then picked up the phone line accessing directly to the Dean's office.

'Sir, some student here to see you,' she said softly. After a second, she placed the mouthpiece on her shoulder, still not looking up to see the student. 'What's your name, dear?'

Lot struggled, but managed in the end. 'Lotando Urey, ma'am.'

The secretary reiterated the name into the mouthpiece. She waited a few more seconds and. in a slow faint tone that amazingly reached Lot's ears more than a buzzer would, said, 'Oh, this is that one. I'll send her in.'

She replaced the phone down and looked up for the first time. Lotando felt her ears melting. The secretary's peer from the specs rescaled her whole body calibrating it into a reference level of extra-trepidation.

The secretary stared at her for a while and then frowned. She re-fixed her spectacles and looked down back to her papers.

'You may go in, he is waiting,' she said in a rather rough voice, gesturing at the door panelled to her far right.

Lotando almost doubled over. She picked her heavy feet and walked over to the door. Her whole academic life rolled over her eyes like a motion film. Generally, her university life at MU was all over. She started to think of how she was going to pursue her life after this. Maybe enrol at another college. It was so sickening.

'Ms Urey?' the voice was neither soft nor kind.

Lot looked up. *Oh man, I must be daydreaming to the fullest.* She now sat at a chair staring at the Dean's desk blank minded. The office was modernized by a desktop and a laser printer. An old clock was pasted at seven feet on one wall, which was crammed with panel bookshelves filled with various books. The floor represented a similar coffee brown carpet that was thinner than the one at the secretary's. Two huge window panels showed over the view of an exquisite orchard that was dominated by blooming trees. The evening's late orange sun shone the upper part of the room into a warm view. An extremely huge desk almost covered the area near to the panels backed by a high black leather armchair. A file, the desktop and a picture frame of what was possibly the Dean's wife and children topped the smoothly vanished desk.

The Dean sat with his hands angled at the desk – one suspending dark-lensed glasses with the fingertips as if afraid that they would somehow break. Looking at him made many feel anxious. Being summoned to his office for corrupt reasons wasn't something any student wanted to experience during campus life. For one thing, he didn't suspend students, he gave you the boot, and Lotando thought she was going to be the latest victim in a few minutes' time.

In her three years at the university, she had only seen him maybe five times during particular ceremonies and other non-frequent important assignments. The high rank of authority the students used to see was his second in command, his Assistant and he was one old funny man. Lot wished she was in his office now.

At least last time Debra's sister had dealt with the prostitute ordeal, now there was no way out. She was close to tears. *I must apologize before he begins*, she thought trembling. *If he gives me the boot, maybe I won't feel so bad.*

The Dean gave Lot a brief survey. He had never seen her before, that was for sure – not for real however. The newspapers hadn't really got her picture that well. She was noticeably beautiful, but currently she looked like she wanted to release a flood of tears.

What she has done isn't what any of her kind would do easily, he thought. *Is she one of those religious inclined people?*

'Sir, I'm very sorry,' Lot began, suppressing a heavy sob. Words clogged her thorax.

'Sorry, Ms Urey?' the Dean raised his eyebrows.

'More than sorry, sir, I shouldn't have,' Lot tried to be composed. She formed small fists with her hands that her knuckles went white. *Face it Lotando, you are going to be expelled*, she chastised herself cruelly. 'I shouldn't have snapped at Professor Gaza like that, but you see, you see, she was...' her voice was lanky. 'She sort of accused me of being a prostitute and, and...' She couldn't finish. She stared at the carpet, tears almost trickling out.

'Oh, that,' the Dean sighed.

These words scrapped Lotando's nerves like sandpaper.

He is going to dismiss me just like that? She thought. The Dean's tone had a note of surprise that surprised her even more. She jerked her head up and could barely see because of tears. Amazingly, her emotions took over strongly and they evaporated. However, she felt a chill as the Dean grinned at her.

The Dean heaved another sigh. 'Ms Urey, I called you here to discuss about April.'

Lotando was dazed out of breath. *April? What about April?* She gazed at him. *Was this some kind of a joke? No!* The Dean's face didn't say so. 'Sir, I don't understand.'

The Dean slowly wore his spectacles and grasped the file. He opened it and took a few sheets of paper from it. 'Pastor Rosina, through the *Anglican Christian Embassy Association* sent a messenger with these to me for reference. They are essential participation forms. I received these forms yesterday,' he said and handed them over to Lotando. 'I've discovered that you and Ms Yana Urey volunteered to take part in this camp as MU's Ambassadors, meaning that you are going to be representing the whole university, which will in turn co-sponsor the camp. Since Ms Yana is currently away on an attachment seminar, unattainable at the moment... you see, these papers need to be delivered back to Harare by tomorrow with our signatures. I believe you know what I'm talking about.'

Lot suddenly deduced what he was saying and nodded. 'Without these, we can't go?' she asked expectantly.

'In a way, I'm afraid so, Ms Urey. You can of course go, sponsoring yourselves, but not officially as MU students or Ambassadors,' the Dean replied in a strained low voice. 'But the university could do with being involved in such things if we are to grow a much reputable image. This is a good thing. We need such an exposure, giving us close relations with various religious organisations. Not to mention that this will go a long way to diffuse the biased belief that we have students who dabble in prostitution whilst they are here.'

Lot's heart began faster. The chance she had been waiting for all semester, the *loophole* at last. She didn't want this kind of compelled commitment. It had been the Yana's plan, Yana's audacity and zeal to involve her into this. Right now, she was the one who had all the power to decide about April.

Participating in Youth Association, oh, what a pack of crap, she thought.

'And there are no other alternatives?' she asked excitedly. 'Er – I mean without my cousin sister here to sign her papers as such.'

The Dean sat up. 'Rather, there are two alternatives.' Lot's heart sank. 'It's either you sign your papers and go solo registered as an MU student...,' he paused and gazed at the forms. 'Since you are Ms Yana Urey's close relative, you can sign them for her as her proxy in full confidence that you assume she'll agree a hundred percent. Note that these papers are basically for proof of acquaintance with this university if something happens that may require the university to be involved or acknowledgement, such as proof of having participated in a leadership camp or something – things that may enhance one's CV after uni.'

Neither of these options appealed to her, but the thought of Yana coming back and realizing that there had been a solution then was demounting. This could have a bad effect on their not so solid relationship. She thought about it for a minute struggling to make the right decision, glaring at the forms. She was afraid of keeping the Dean waiting, but his quietness seemed like he didn't mind at all.

The Dean smiled, watching the girl, seeing her anxious. It wasn't a soft decision to make. It was never one when religion was involved, especially to this new generation. He was glad he didn't have to make a decision for someone else for once. Lot saw some new columns on the forms. *Do you like to be a team leader?* This was on both forms. She grinned. *Payback time.*

'I'll sign both of them, sir, if you don't mind,' she alleged with a sigh.

The Dean observed her thoughtfully. 'So you don't doubt a bit about Ms Yana's choice, Ms Urey?'

'No, sir, it was in fact her idea. I wouldn't want to disappoint her.'

'Very well,' he said cheerfully and handed her a silver pen. 'You can go ahead.'

In five minutes, they had both gone over the papers' signing phase her own copies in hand. Lotando was feeling a little better, trying not to think that she had actually shared a pen with the Dean. This was wild. When they had finished, Lot was about to leave the room when the Dean stopped her. *What now?*

'Er – by the way, Ms Urey, please try not to get a little impatient with Professor Gaza,' his tone was pleasantly laughing. 'She has been bothering since Wednesday about you.'

CHAPTER EIGHT

Proposed Role

During mid-March, the campus was getting too hot for Lot. Since that heated lecture, Professor Gaza always had something to say about the disrespectful youth of today. Lotando cared less and ignored her twittering. She had been lucky last time. She wasn't going to push her luck. Being in the Dean's office signing papers was one thing, being called there for other reasons was another she didn't want to get herself involved in. So far, two political activist students had packed their bags for good that semester. Everyone was scared to do anything out of the ordinary. There was no return ticket to exit. Lot felt glad she wasn't one of them.

As she did no active sports, Lotando kept herself fit through *jogging hour*. This was her friends' programmed health session. They had formulated it during the first year after Debra had come across a health tip article in a so-called magazine. They had formed a three-member group that constantly kept tight exercise schedules on Wednesday afternoons. The program included jogging around the campus after lessons and sit-ups. Many had stopped wondering why these three always looked so damn fit and beautiful. Some many more had copied from them. Amazingly, to the three, Yana had joined the crew. They were currently helping each other, taking turns on sit-ups.

'This feels good,' Yana said out of breath. 'I'm actually straining my –'

'Cut the anatomy, Doc!' Debra jeered, holding Yana's straight legs firmly to the ground. 'This is no Physiology 101.' The others laughed. 'Anyway, why the sudden interest in joining us youngsters? Last year you called us *guy wannabes,* Doc.'

'I'm trying to remain young and stay fit,' Yana breathed as she reclined. She panted as she came up for a sit up. 'Physical composure is critical to ability success.'

'Here we go again,' Fadzai called out. She was struggling to finish the second phase of a sixty press up. 'All chatty chatty again, damn! What is it with all you med students and trying to show off the little you know?'

'Expertise beats stupidity, my dear Fadzi,' Yana blew. The other girls giggled.

'Any more of that snappy crap from you, you'll be *Grey's Anatomying* yourself soon, Doc,' Fadzai groaned and knelt after a successful, but tiring phase.

The others laughed. A couple of wolf whistles came from a distance. They stared in that direction and saw a group of distinguishable male final years passing by, short and medium, tall, handsome and burly.

'Want some help, ladies?' a tall dude cried.

'Assist yourself by walking away with your baby giraffes, Mr Giraffe,' Fadzi retorted, glaring at the crew. The dudes laughed. Fadzi eyed the effortlessly attracted Debra eyeing them. That meant trouble. 'We have got our boyfriends watching,' she added giving Debra a nasty nudge to wake her up.

'Who cares?' one of them dared to come close. He was wearing a black and white shirt over a blue T-shirt. His jeans fitted him well, and his sneakers looked marvellously white, like they were just from the shop.

Damn, he looks cool, Debra thought smiling.

He deposited himself close by, sitting on a fixed recess stone.

'Didn't you hear us, wimp?' Fadzi barked out, glaring at him. *Boy, he seems delectable.* 'I said we don't want your help. Why don't you be a nice puppy and follow your dogs,' she said pointing at the other pack now a distance away.

'Who said I wanted to help?' the guy smirked. His head was covered by a black cap making his eyes inconspicuous. He looked younger, as if he could be a freshman. His white teeth flashed against his medium complexioned skin. 'I wanna watch.'

Fadzi fumed. 'Watch – are you mental?'

'Hey, Lot and Nana, you never told me that you had such a waspy gorgeous friend?' the guy suddenly said, taking off his cap and exposing fine short cut hair. Fadzi was dumbfounded.

CHAPTER NINE

Semester Fever

Yana picked her notebook and stood up. She replaced the chair and strolled over to the leisure reading bookshelves. The library was exceedingly huge and modern. Whatever subject you wanted to read, you would find it in there.

At three in the afternoon, and on a Friday on the 23rd of March, the library was scarcely populated. Not many cared to read in it at that time of the semester. Lot watched her replacing an old volume of the King James Version Bible at the religious section and slumped.

She is done, she thought, *and I haven't even started.*

She felt her anger well up as Yana waved goodbye from the main desk as she checked out. Lot imagined all the fun her friends were probably having in town if they hadn't gotten themselves into another drama. She gritted her teeth.

Such times with chums mustn't be missed, she thought. She worked her long hair and stared back into her Bible. She was opening the book of Psalms.

Psalms iii
<u>*Praise the Lord*</u>
I will extol the Lord with all my heart in the council of the upright and in the assembly.

She half understood what these words meant. Once she had tried to *believe* and once she had *believed*. It was in the past now and none of it no longer made sense to her. She slammed the New International Version Bible shut after a few minutes, including her notebook, which absolutely had nothing resourceful in it. She strolled over to the religious section and replaced the Bible on the rightful shelf.

'Why do we have to do this, Yana?' Lotando asked, taking a small sip from her drink bottle.

The soda tasted good on her taste buds. She sipped feverishly. Only two weeks were left and the other part of the semester was going to be long gone. *Her final lectures and exams after the Easter holidays were going to be something really*, she speculated, especially the ones involving BMP. She had a feeling BMP was going to fail her that semester.

'For fun and for religious faith – not to mention community service credit for our resumes,' Yana spoke briefly. She was going over an edition of a Hardy Boys Mystery 3in1 hardback. Her life was ending really cool at MSM. *Only a semester to go and I am Dr Yana Urey*, she laughed despite herself.

'And that's actually supposed to be funny?' Lot snapped.

'No,' Yana simply answered. She flipped over a page and continued reading.

MU's recreational park was unusually peaceful and a light cool breeze moistened the early evening's atmosphere. Suddenly, Lot looked up and saw someone coming toward them. She grinned at him. He only smiled back.

'Lady and Dr,' he said. 'What a pleasure to see you two, just the people I was dying to see all day.'

'And why is that, *Ash?*' Yana held, without taking her eyes from the novel. 'Short of hommies?'

'Since we are going to be sticking together like ants next month, I might as well start hanging with you. I'm the only guy representing MU, you know.'

'Good for you,' Lot smirked. The Dean had claimed they were only two of them – the Ureys – standing out for MU. He had meant the females and she hadn't known until only week ago.

Ash sat next to Yana and peered into her novel. 'What are you reading, Nana?'

Yana thrust the book into his face, angered at being interrupted.

'Hardy Boys?' Ash sighed reclining on the lawn. 'I used to love those when I was a boy.'

'What happened?' Yana quipped. 'Grew too much hair to be a

boy anymore?'

Ash laughed. 'Maybe, what about you?' Lotando joined in the laughter as Yana frowned.

A soft silence flowed through the air for a while. Ash whistled slowly. Lot casually lay on her back on the lawn, her cap shading her eyes from the feeble sun. She felt her muscles strain from the stress of preparing for their upcoming late May exams.

'Are you prepared, everything ready with your presentations and stuff?' Lotando whispered.

'I heard that,' Yana informed cheerfully.

'Whatever you hear is no secret, Nana,' Lot said.

'My stuff has been cool since I started attending church service as a toddler. I'll use my common knowledge with some help from the *Big Book*,' Ash replied confidently. 'It's not exactly an exam, you know – you don't need to study or worry much about it.'

Lotando groaned. *Nice answer, Ash. At least I'm not the only one who doesn't feel so up to this.*

'Where are the others?' Ash suddenly asked.

Lotando rotated her head toward him without lifting it from the ground and gazed at him confused. 'What others?'

'Your girls – the other two hot ones,' he whispered to her. Yana's eyes gleamed at her novel, but she said nothing. Ash thought she had heard nothing as intended. He sighed in relief.

'They went out for the Friday, and will probably be back before five, I think,' Lot whispered back. *If they don't get involved amongst another group of prostitutes, that is.*

'Went out, hey?'

'Not like what you are thinking, Ash, not like that. You should know better that I don't do things like that,' Lot's voice was disappointed.

'Of course I know, only asking,' he grinned avoiding her glare.

'Why?' Yana suddenly asked. 'Why ask about them?'

'Maybe you could help me out, Doc, you are a lady too. Right?' Ash sat up and snatched the novel from Yana's grasp. A page ripped in the process.

Yana screamed and rose to her feet. Ash sided a few meters from her angry reach. Lot remained resting between them, giggling. *Serves you right for meddling into other people's conversations,* she noted.

'Give me that back or I'll kick your ass, Ash, now!' Yana fumed her hands in akimbo.

'Lovely language you got there, Doc. I'm not giving you back this teenager's book, not until you agree to help me out, please sit down, let us discuss.'

Yana's face was firm with anger, but she saw no way of forcing Ash to her will. He would simply run away and toy with her for the rest of the evening. Her mind told her to cool down and retaliate later. She sat down forever trying to calm down. Lot remained as quiet as if she didn't exist.

'Good!' Ash said soothingly, but remained standing. 'Thank you, Nana.'

'So what is this thing you want the Doc to help you on?' Lot giggled the question out.

'You can help too, Lot. After all you know her better,' Ash replied grimacing.

Know who? Lot thought curiously.

'I can't take my mind off her since that day, all that fury and everything. I think I've fallen in love, very superhot attached,' Ash said in a sad puppy lovesick manner.

He sat back on the ground and returned the Hardy Boys to Yana who was no longer interested in it. Yana glared at him, smiling. She really did want to hear this.

'Who are you talking about?' Yana crooned.

'She has got my mind dreaming of endless romance stories, resuscitating my infatuation in an endless ego. She has got me biting my fingernails –'

'Hey, dude! Who is this person?' Yana cried impatiently, but all fell to no ears.

Ash was gazing down like a boy about to cry after being refused some candy. 'And I don't know how to tell her or know if she feels the same. I'm a part four varsity student, that old, but I've never done these kind of things you know and –'

Yana cracked his forehead with the Hardy Boys. He woke up seemingly surprised.

'Who is it?' Lotando asked curiously now sitting straight.

Ash finally looked up. 'It's you, Lot,' he said without trying to reserve any emotion.

'What?' the Ureys cried out.

Lot's heart seemed to stop. *This can't be insanely true.* This wasn't something she hadn't bargained for all her life. It was totally unfit. The puzzle didn't have pieces. *He must be mad.*

'I just can't stop myself,' Ash leaned over eyes closing to give a good kiss expecting to receive a full one.

Their mouths drew closer and Yana groaned and closed her eyes. *So, so unbelievable*, Yana thought stunned even to look. People at campus kissed all the time, but not Lot, *not in a million years,* and yet she closed her eyes tighter not wanting to see it to believe it.

Smooch! People who kissed in passion didn't produce smacks. Yana's eyes flashed open. *Unbelievable!* Ash had planted a kiss on Lot's cheek again and they were hugging, briefly looking at her.

That's it? Yana thought amazed. *A kiss on the cheek and huggy huggy? Or you kids, you are so kids.*

'Got you, Nana!' Ash cried in laughter.

'What?'

'I promised I'd get you back one day, Yana. Wow – I did it,' Ash was very excited. 'You should have seen your face.'

'So what was that all about?' Yana asked stunned.

'Play acting, Doc. I told Lot the name when I gave her a perk.'

'No, you didn't!'

'I whispered it to her,' Ash said with a proud tone.

'You two are so horrible,' Yana cried in anguish.

She felt so angry about being kept in a curious end. Another half hour passed with Yana giving them a piece of her mind. Lot wasn't listening.

What a shocker, she thought of Ash's sudden infatuation. *I wonder how she feels in turn, and balmy, my feet are wet.*

CHAPTER TEN

The Days

Lloyd Urey stared over the empty client's chair. He breathed in heavily. It was seven in the evening and he was still in his Belgravia office practically doing nothing. In his life, he had learned to master the art of manipulating people to gain wealth. His plans were graduated by perfection, increasing with each plan executed. He wondered if the plan he was currently working on was going to come out as good as the others. It was by far no ordinary venture. He left the office so unsure. Easter was only a few days away.

'Daddy, we can very well take care of ourselves.'

'I know that very well, Yana,' Mr Urey stood his ground. Yana's fiery stare doubled over his confidence. She looked very much like her mother. From hair to toe, except for those eyes, they genetically shared those. Those fearless intelligent eyes.

The Ureys' lounge had never felt so cold, Lot thought. The lounge was big enough to be a millionaire's saloon. The centre had a glass table and small glass stools. A huge fruit bowl encircled the middle of the table. The two ladies were currently sitting at a sofa facing Mr Urey who was standing on the brink of the fireplace. This was almost something as close to a 10 P.M. lecture as you could get, Lotando thought frowning. Her nightclothes felt scrappy on her cold skin. She took an apple from the fruit collection and bit a huge chunk from it. Her uncle glared at her and frowned at the crunching sound. Lot arched a brow in an apologizing manner.

'As I was saying –' Mr Urey continued.

Yana took an apple and gave it a wholesome noisy bite. Lot knew she did this purposefully to annoy the man. Mr Urey's ears turned red. He stepped over and was about to say something undeniably bitter. Incredibly, he stopped. He stared at the two. Yana was trying hard to chew the big piece she had bitten whilst Lot nibbled her apple in embarrassment.

Mr Urey looked up at the watch and grinned. He picked up a greener apple from the bowl and polished it with the sleeve of his *who knew dollars expensive suit's* jacket. He gave it an after sniff, tossed it up in the air twice and took a smaller bite.

The ladies glared at him incredulously. Uncle Urey continued to chew bits by bit of his apple in slit mechanization. Lot looked at the clock.. *So late to be having a competition of eating apples,* she thought. She looked back at her uncle and her cousin sister and knew the deal. *If you don't want to listen, I won't talk until you want me to.*

'Okay, Uncle, what is it you were saying?' she started, knowing Mr Urey and Yana to both be too determined to compete for dominance until six in the morning. By then no fruit would be left in the bowl.

Mr Urey smiled. *That wasn't so bad, was it?* He gazed appealingly at Lot, who grinned back at him. Yana gave a soft frustrated phew.

'Should a father or uncle be wrong to worry about his daughter's or niece's welfare, Yana?' Mr Urey asked.

'No, father, but should you worry that much to wake us up at ten in the night?' Yana emphasized.

'Yeah, we may die due to lack of sleep, Uncle.' Lot added subconsciously and yawned.

'Ok then,' he said indifferently. 'Good night.' He left them gaping.

Just like that? Lotando thought heatedly. She hated mysteries, especially the ones involving her uncle. Lot had a difficult time suppressing Yana from cursing aloud as they headed up for their bedrooms. Suddenly, she no longer felt sleepy.

That Sunday, less than a week before they were *game*, Lotando spent most of her time in the garden trying to compose a very good presentation of what she was going possibly to offer.

She didn't like it at all. Even Winster was finding the going get suck. Not everyone was enjoying this, she bet. She had to read over the holiday and her course studies were becoming as wearisome as ever. Easter was due that Friday.

'Hi!' Yana cried out, banging out of the kitchen door into the garden.

Lotando unenthusiastically looked up from her Bible and waved her nearly ink empty pen at her. 'Hi, Nana.'

''Where is Win, I thought he was somewhere around you.'

'No, I'm alone here,' Lot shrugged.

It was one in the afternoon and it was obvious that Winster was somewhere in the hood, at the Dotonas' or where else, but the Hewstones. Under normal circumstances, Yana never looked for Winster for anything, which made this rather unusual.

Yana surveyed the whole garden from the door calling Winster by his nickname, then after a while in frustration by his real name. She got no results.

'Where can he be? I've been looking all over for him for about –'

'As you can see, he isn't here,' Lot frowned, trying to re-concentrate back at her Bible. She jotted down a few notes to work on hoping Yana would suddenly get on.

'Why so testy?' Yana suddenly stared down at her. 'Need any help with those?'

'I can manage, Doc,' Lot heated. 'Piss off and leave me in peace.'

Yana shrugged. 'I only wanted to help.'

Lot almost rose up in fury. 'If you really wanted to help me, Nana, you could have handsomely done so long ago without failure. You could have left me out of this shit.'

Yana looked heartbroken. 'But it will be lots of fun. I thought you would somehow feel the same. You signed our papers with the Dean.'

Perfect! Lotando thought. *And I thought I was being civil.* 'You're looking for Win, why don't you just call him on his cell?'

'Winster barely carries that thing with him. Wonder why father wasted his time and money buying him one.'

'Oh,' Lot sighed and remained silent for a while. 'Please go, Nana – before I lose my temper.'

'Okay, I am gone.' And she was gone.

The cool evening wavered in calm breezes, cumulating the sky into an overcast, but relaxing mood. Yana and Lotando were returning from Father Rosina's expecting to be updated on their forthcoming expedition, but they had hit a dead duck. It being a Sunday, the pastor was away for the whole day. The two decided to take a walk in their street for a while enjoying the fresh air.

'There he is, look!' Yana suddenly exclaimed pointing at one of the road's terraces. Winster was emerging from the Hewstones' electrical gate accompanied by two girls and an older beautiful young lady.

Lotando giggled badly. The three girls gave her curious glares. 'Way to go, Win,' she whispered to Yana.

'Hi, Yana,' the Hewstone girls said simultaneously. '… and Lotando,' they added hesitantly, feeling uncomfortable by Lot's ceaseless giggles.

'Hi, you two,' Yana nudged Lot who reiterated the words to greet the Hewstone sisters.

'Hi, ladies,' the young lady crooned handing something to Winster in a secretive manner.

Lot was very curious by this gesture. This was the first time she had ever seen the girl and Winster in each other's company. Winster grinned at her and stuffed the tiny sheet of paper into his pocket.

'Chenai,' Yana excitedly hugged the girl. 'Long time no see. How is your after-school experience coming along?'

'Boring,' Chenai said in a good-natured way. 'I can't wait to join you two at MU in summer. Hi, Lot.' The two hugged.

'That will be you two from this summer,' Yana informed excitedly. 'I've had enough of MU.'

'Oh, I had forgotten that you finish this semester – that's so cool.'

'Got me wishing I was her,' Winster added, trying to get as far away from Lotando as he could.

He knew exactly what she was thinking of doing and he couldn't afford to risk it. Lot was so daring with him. There was no telling what she would do.

'Keep on wishing, muffin,' Yana said. 'I was looking for you all morning, where were you?' she added remembering. She gazed at the Hewstone sisters then at Chenai and grinned. 'Oh, silly me, please don't answer.'

Winster shrugged. 'Why were you looking for me?'

'There is this friend of yours called Joshua, he came by at ten – nice guy.' Yana told him.

Winster groaned. 'I'll call him, thanks for playing secretary, Nana.'

Yana aimed a slap at his head. Winster ducked in time and drifted away to a safer distance. 'You say something like that again and I'll shave your hair off no matter who is there to witness it.'

The other girls laughed. Win squared in embarrassment and said nothing knowing his sister too well to try turning jokes into practical experiments. The group found a nice spot and sat there chatting the day off.

A pink Bentley suddenly skirted into the lane. A stunning young woman sat beautifully behind the wheel. The Hewstone sisters demonstratively grimaced. The car parked right in front of them.

'*Bonsoir*,' the beauty cried to the group. Her lightened expression suddenly faded as she saw Yana. 'Oh, it's you.'

'Who did you think it was, Oprah?' Yana scolded.

'Cool it, Nana,' Lot muttered under her breath.

'I didn't know Oprah to be so tall and cunning,' the lady glazed back at her. 'Since when did reality shows entertain braincases.'

The Bentley's passenger door suddenly beeped open. 'She doesn't mean that, Nana.'

'You?' Yana struggled to catch her breath, furious and surprised. 'What the hell are you doing in her car, Ash?'

'And why would that be any of your business?' the beauty snapped.

'Guess what, Brenla? He is my new boyfriend. Does that register in your dimwit cerebrum?' Yana stood up and went directly to face her.

Brenla opened her door and challenged the Urey lady, by resoundingly slamming the door shut behind her. The others stared in silence.

'Don't make me laugh. What are you now, a sugar mummy?' Brenla shouted.

'A what?'

'Yana, please just ignore her. Let it be,' Lotando whispered fiercely.

This wasn't a day to become nasty. Yana amazingly cooled down on her command and was about to let it be, turning away.

'That's funny. You are actually taking orders from the *lovers' path entertainer*,' Brenla mocked.

'Now look here you –' Lot was up on her feet in a flash.

Ash caught hold of her just in time and swung her away. 'Hey, hey chill, Lot.' He whisked her away from the group in the direction of their houses. 'Thanks for the ride, Bren!' he shouted over his shoulder.

'Any time, Tawanda,' Brenla shouted back.

She gave Yana one last fierce glare and inserted herself back into her car. Her sisters jumped in the back and front and the car was off. It swerved into the thoroughfare and entered the Hewstones' Estate.

'You should have let me give her a black eye,' Lot seethed.

'Not healthy, next week we are going to be together, remember?' Tawanda claimed glancing at Chenai to Win. Chenai blushed. He smiled back. 'That wasn't a better start.'

'Who gives a damn about that, Ash?' Yana put in. She put her hands onto her brother's shoulder. 'We are surely going to have some fun, aren't we?' she quipped.

Lotando looked at her. She saw Yana gaze at Chenai then at Winster, same with Tawanda. Tawanda and Yana looked at each other and grinned. Lotando got the picture and smiled. *Some fun that was going to be,* she grinned too.

CHAPTER ELEVEN

Rush Hour

The Park's diluted oxygen and carbon dioxide blew swiftly with the westerly airflow. It passed over the wide artificial surface and rose perpendicularly, then after an insidious climb, fell onto the leeward side onto the stone.

Tiny moisture droplets mixed with the air forcing it to circle the trees. As the air circled the camping site, it licked many Stone and Iron Age archaeological remains. Several Wilton artefacts, including polished implements, shook from the wind's pressure vibrating echoes to the epic centre, rebounding waves that rose upwards then outwards like the ascending winds of a tropical cyclone at the vortex.

The forest presented primly fresh vegetation cleared by the wilderness scavengers. Clear paths marked the hinges of the vegetation at variable angles. Huge mountains bore caves protruding in every sector. A distance away going in the south-west direction, a beautifully laid plain entertained a windmill.

The *farmer* blew his nose and inhaled a huge packet of air. It smelt good. It tasted good. Rain was near. He strolled back into the farmhouse to go to bed. He grinned. His wife was waiting.

Grandma Urey gazed at her *visitor*. She felt uneasy, but there was still nothing she could do. *If Chris was still here*, she thought sadly, *perhaps things would be different*. It was a matter of mysteries. She knew them to be that horrid, *"never enchanting"* as her granddaughter used to philosophize.

'How long will it take?' she asked. She placed her cup of tea on the tea table.

'About twenty-one days to be precise, which will be more than enough.'

She wriggled uncomfortably in her soft chair. 'Is it really that necessary?'

'Very!' the visitor said firmly. 'Very necessary, it must be the only way to find out about *her*.'

'What about this man you chose to handle this situation. Is he that solid?'

'I don't have any fears on him. He is more than capable,' the visitor pompously emphasized.

'So why am I to know all this?' Grandma Urey sniffed and popped her brows.

'You always wanted to know the truth, didn't you?' the visitor said in a firm voice. 'That there is something different about this girl and what the old man died knowing. You too want to know, don't you?'

'But knowing and doing what you are suggesting are two different things. I don't see the meaning of doing what you want to,' Grandma Urey was anxious.

'Sometimes, to get the best of results, extraordinary out of the box things have to happen. You know that, you've always taught me that.'

'Yes, but –' Grandma Urey let it take off. 'There is something you don't know.'

The visitor shrugged and rose from the chair. The visitor paced back and forth, striding jealous strides. The silence stretched out for two whole minutes.

'What is it?' the visitor finally asked sceptically.

'First, you have to promise me something, before I tell you,' Grandma Urey's voice was weak. She had the visitor make a few promises.

Another exasperating silence stirred for several minutes. 'It is hard for me to say this, but...' Grandma Urey offered at last.

The commuter minibus terminus was dynamic at that moment in time. It was at peak hour when people rushed for transport from the CBD for home. The daylight however took its time to sleep away. A couple of months ago, the time could have been mistaken for three in the afternoon. A sweet young woman boarded a white and red bus. It was three quarters full. She hastily looked around for a vacant seat. There were five available. She liked one and a *wink* gave her the motivation. She went and placed herself in the seat trying to look absent-minded.

'Hi,' the guy sitting beside her said.

The lady stared at him and smiled. 'Hi,' she held out her palm.

'Busy day?'

The lady was confused. 'Excuse me?'

'I said, it's been a pretty hot day, hasn't it?' the guy grinned. 'You look flushed.'

The lady laughed. 'Oh, sorry, who else wouldn't?' she said, holding a bunch of textbooks in the air.

'Bookworm?'

The lady blushed. 'Not exactly, I just try to be one.'

The guy laughed this time looking at the front of the bus. It was filling up. *Good*, he thought, *nobody familiar*. He couldn't bear the thought of being seen boarding a *kombi*.

Anyway, it has its benefits, he thought eyeing the pretty lady. 'I've never seen you before, do you live in Chizz?'

The lady shook her head. 'Nah, I'm visiting for Easter. My sister's new place that is.'

'Ah, cool!' he said, gazing out of the window. The bus was eventually on its course. He suddenly jerked up. 'Oh my, where are my manners. Silly me! My name is Never Dotona.'

The lady smiled. *I have heard that name before,* she thought. *Where, when and from whom?* She looked at him curiously. He was staring back at her as if waiting for something. She suddenly remembered. 'Oh, sorry, I'm Debra Queen Swera,' she copied the way he had introduced himself.

They both laughed and it was ever so pleasant.

'You're indeed a Queen if I might say,' Never complemented.

Debra was flattered. 'Please don't tease me. I'm not anything close to that. A simple girl would be more like it.' They both laughed again.

The bus drove leaving the CBD into the adjacent suburbs.

'Where actually in Chizz will you be staying, if you don't mind me asking?' Never inquired. The girl had such a lovely laugh, soothing and merry.

Debra raised a brow. 'Er – I'm not actually that familiar with the place, it's somewhere close to Harare Drive, it's in Dover Rd.'

'Oh!'

'What?'

'Nothing, Dover Road is at the backyard of my neighbourhood,' Never informed nonchalantly.

'Somewhere near Stopford Close,'

'Yeah, how did you know?' Never was startled.

'Well, one of my friends lives there,' Debra said grandly with a broad grin.

'Who may that be, Yana?' Never mused, his voice amused.

Debra shook her head slightly. 'Not Nana, Lotando Urey.'

Never smiled and gave her books a curious glare. 'You are an electrical comp wizard as well, I mean comp witch.'

'No!' Debra said. She handed him one of her books. 'I'm majoring in Political Science.'

Never was taken aback. 'Ah, a politician, you got me worrying.'

'Please don't, I'll not analyse you,' Debra laughed.

Never smiled back and flipped the book over. Half of the things in it he half understood. 'You know, can you do me a favour?'

Debra raised her eyebrows and bit her lip again. 'What?'

'Can you give me an analysis on someone familiar?' Never said, looking directly at her. 'Can you, please?'

'Shoot away,' Debra was eager.

'Analyse Lotando for me.'

Debra's lightened expression faded slightly. *And here I thought you were interested in me.*

Never saw her look and added quickly. 'I mean, I barely have an idea who she really is. Yana, that one I do know.'

'Why?' Debra asked, now very curious. 'I need to ask her first before I publicize such info. I'll be seeing her on Saturday.'

'You wouldn't do that, she would…' Never began, unnerved by the suggestion. 'Anyway I don't think you'll be seeing her on Saturday.'

'What do you mean?' Debra asked. 'Where will she be? She told me she would be at home all Easter holiday.'

Never shrugged. *Very neat, Lot,* he thought with a sigh. *Next time, please don't make such pretty friends and not tell them about your whereabouts.* He looked at her. She was waiting and he knew he had to tell her if he needed the favour returned.

CHAPTER TWELVE

The Journey

'Ms Urey, please sign here and pass the pad around.'

Lotando received the pen, pad, and stared at its blue sheet of paper. It smelt nice. She had a brief look and saw their names neatly printed in with a space on the right hand side vacant for the signatures. She scribbled her somewhat long signature and had another brief look at the paper.

All their names were truly there. She passed it on to Brenla who took it in a huff and used her own expensive silver pen to sign. All signed the documentation and handed the pad back to him. Father Rosina made a swift verification noting each signature. He finally signed his own signature and entered into the bus. A few moments after the driver and medical assistant had signed the form, Father Rosina reappeared.

'Everything is in order. I'll deposit the original copy at the Cathedral in town on our way through,' he said. He held the pad up stamping the form tight on its surface. 'As I call your name, you'll board the bus. Just procedure, Ms Hewstone, please don't frown.'

Brenla looked up, blushing. She gave her travel bag a soft pat and placed it in front of her.

'Ms Lotando Urey.'

Lotando heaved her bags and inserted herself into the bus. She chose her sitting spot instantly and drew her stuff over without hesitation.

'Ms Brenla Hewstone.'

Brenla struggled to get her suitcase through the door, but later managed with the help of the medic asst. She chose a seat close to the door and far from the Urey lady.

'Ms Chenai Muchemwa.'

Chenai carried her belongings with ice cream ease. She gazed throughout the bus. It was huge, enough to exchange seats when fatigue approached her later. She chose the long back seat for space.

'Mr Jack Dotona.'

The fat boy had to use all his flesh to carry his belongings, refusing any help from the medic assistant. He sat midway on the right side of the bus, just a few meters from Lotando's seat.

'Mr Godfrey Hewstone.'

Godfrey carried himself with athletic ease and went to sit on the back seat with Chenai. The two started chatting, a nice picture according to Lot, and an unpleasant one to Brenla who frowned at him. She had been hoping that he would have kept her company up front.

'Mr Never Dotona.'

Never picked his broad suitcase and boarded the bus. He looked around and picked up Lot. To Lotando's and almost a wishful Brenla's surprise, he went and sat beside Lot. Lotando blushed as he said *"hi"*. Brenla glared her knife-edges in thousands.

'Mr Tawanda Muchemwa.'

Tawanda carried his flexible, three loaded backpack luggage and jumped into the bus. He looked expectantly where Lotando was sitting and shuddered. *Oh damn you boy,* he thought fiercely.

Tawanda gazed around and finally settled beside Brenla. Brenla beamed with joy. They immediately started their own fluffy conversation. The medic assistant grinned at their lovely picture. *They look so perfect,* he thought. His *hopes* faded shortly.

'Ms Yana Urey.'

Yana heated up, furious at being kept waiting, carried her suitcase and backpack with the help of the medic assistant. Realizing there was nowhere suitable to fit herself, she placed her bags behind Lotando and Never and then returned to sit with the medic assistant upfront.

There will be lots in common there, Tawanda and Lot thought at the sight of the medic assistant and to-be physician getting into familiar terms with each other.

'And finally, Mr Winster Urey. Let me help you with that, Mr Urey.'

Winster had wisely chosen his luggage. Only two heavy backpacks with all that he needed.

'Excellent!' Father Rosina said excitedly, getting into the bus and standing upfront looking at them all from the driver's view. The bus's door electrically swung shut. 'I'll make a few introductions. Our driver is going to be Mr Legondo and our medical assistant, Dr Derrick Mwanza. Mr Legondo, we may proceed.'

The bus left for the city centre. After Father Rosina had submitted the legal papers at the Cathedral, the bus headed East.

CHAPTER THIRTEEN

Easter Bearing

Mr Legondo accelerated and had the needle fluctuate between 80-90km/hr. On Saturdays, the lengthy Marondera Road was as busy as ever, especially with it being a holiday when kids got exchanged from relative to relative.

This also being the harvesting season, so many buses were probably loading bumper harvests from the countryside to the cities. He remembered himself being in that kind of trade before, the clever inspectors to deal with en route, the traffic police to evade and the numerous bus conductors to befriend. At least now, he had a stable position and a lucrative one as well. He was feasting on congregational benefits and he loved being a *newborn*. His life was now pure. Anyway, this trip was going to be more fun, more like a three-week holiday in the mountains. He was expected to check into a hotel for the whole period they were going to be there. He thought of what he was going to do with his time to kill. He had no brilliant ideas. He wished he could have brought his wife.

What am I going to be doing with all that time? He thought.

Some fun, my man, your old kind of fun.

No, I don't do those kinds of things anymore, he slighted off the thought.

Only this once —

No! No! No…

'Hey?'

He felt a soft pat on the shoulder. He flinched and abruptly woke up from his thoughts. He was sweating, he noticed.

'I'm sorry. How is it going?'

Mr Legondo looked up and saw the pastor looking down at him with comfortable eyes. 'Smoothly, Father, this is one hot day,' he claimed, wiping his brow.

'I have a dilemma with the study of people's attitudes towards people with disabilities. I had to skip that segment one semester. I don't understand the sequences, I get too emotional.'

'Well, Ms Urey –'

'Please call me Yana.'

'Well, Yana, that's a simple course to do because it's very realistic and sensitively based. Firstly, you need to define what *attitudes* are. According to Byrne, I think, Attitude is enduring mental representations of various features of the social or physical world. They are acquired through experience and degree a directive influence on subsequent behaviour,' Derrick used his intellectual matureness in explaining.

'Defining the issue is one thing, explaining the attitude is another.'

Derrick smiled at her. She was extremely pretty to become a doctor. When Pastor Rosina had told him about her, he actually hadn't expected to see someone like her.

'If I'm to quote a 1993 Paris line, I'd say it's based upon negative attitudes. There are less positive ones if I may say. Negative attitudes may be had in situations like their influence in the decisions directed towards funding. They may also influence the attitude of healthcare students like you, thus perpetuating a negative image of disabled people isn't very different from those of the general public and may become more negative as professional education proceeds.'

Yana gazed at him amused. 'How old are you, Derrick?'

Ouch! Derrick stared at her. 'Twenty four and a half,'

'Oh my, boy you are so learned.' They laughed.

Brenla gazed at the picture. The lady was perfectly scanned onto an A5 paper. Brenla smiled taking a closer look. 'Wow, what's her name?'

'Fadzai – what are your comments?'

Brenla grinned. 'She looks awesome, that I must truly say.'

'Wish she was more like you though.'

Brenla beamed. 'Now what is that supposed to mean?' she

leaned on his shoulder. 'Are you having second thoughts about us, Tawa?'

Tawanda soothed her hair. 'No, why would I? You aren't having them yourself, are you?'

'That's cute,' Brenla laughed taking her head off his shoulder.

Tawanda joined in the laughter. Lotando looked curiously in their direction. She felt waxed.

'Did you really mean it, Bren, is she that cool?' Tawa asked.

Brenla produced some kind of expensive-looking lovely juice from her bag and sipped. 'Your possible new girlfriend is beautiful, kind of makes me a little jealous. You have an elevated taste in women. Thirsty?' she said, offering him her bottle forever smiling and sparkling.

'Yeah, thanks.' He took it and it went directly to his mouth.

What? Lotando and Yana gawked unbelievably. He hadn't even attempted to wipe off the wrench's saliva. *Yuck,* they thought.

Tawanda drank the bottle downwards. Brenla snatched it from his mouth just in time. 'Hey, I didn't say you could ice your windpipe like that with my sweet juice. Oh, you are horrible. Rule number one – never treat a lady like that otherwise…'

Tawanda laughed. 'Yeah, I get it,' he said drying his t-shirt from some of the juice that had dropped onto it after Brenla had yanked her bottle.

'Let me read her before you tell me about her,' Brenla crooned. 'Can I?'

'As if I'd stop you, sis, let's see if you really know people as I think you don't.'

Brenla smiled studying the picture more. 'She must be freaky if pissed, a bee, waspy and quite shy if foreign and a serious one for cool long relationships. She has probably gone through one boyfriend in the past or…' her smile broadened. '… none, you might be Mr *First*. For a girl her age, that seems quite rare.'

Tawanda smiled. *Glad you did read her.*

'Don't be awed, I'm a CEO remember. I deal with people, it's part of my job description,' Brenla bragged.

'OMG!' Tawanda chuckled and smiled a while.

He looked upfront and saw Yana glaring at him. Her stare was cold. He felt himself sinking into his seat. 'Now, tell me what you have been up to lately,' he looked back at Brenla. Brenla fired away.

Lotando barely heard the words of her companion. They were very faint, scarcely registering. She wished she were daydreaming. She was jealous and she didn't try to deny that feeling in her. *How could Ash click so marvellously with Brenla, the enemy?* The way they exchanged strokes, it was all fascinating. It was exactly the way they almost did, Lot and he, only that Brenla wasn't afraid or shy to be more physical. She couldn't bear the thought that the arrogant bitch could be as much as a friend to Ash as her or Yana.

'You got a thing for Ashley?' This sentence did go through.

'Sorry!' she jerked startled. She looked beside her and saw Never staring at her curiously with a friendly smile. 'What did you say?'

'You heard me, Lot. Don't answer if you don't want to,' he laughed.

He was so at ease and calm that Lotando had no idea why he had come along this trip. There were much more important, much cooler, things for Never Dotona to do than waste his time doing this.

'Oh, I'm sorry,' Lotando answered.

'Stop apologizing, Lot. Why apologize to me? You have done me no wrong.'

Lot smiled. The guy was an ass to Yana because he liked to *bling*, but he wasn't that bad. In fact, he was the coolest talking dude Lot had ever come across. *Maybe that's why all the girls Yana would think are childish or slutty like him,* she thought. She indeed felt like liking him now.

'I got nothing for Tawanda,' she answered after a while. 'Don't get me wrong, we are just friends.'

'Really?'

'Really, Never, we are just friends,' Lotando said more firmly.

Never saw the look on her face. She had a sudden stunning change of facial expressions that made her look devastatingly attractive. It was hard to read anything about her feelings. Debra had said as much.

'So why look at him and Bren like that?' Never asked with an annoying laugh.

'I just don't like Bren and the idea of her talking to one of the people I like doesn't appeal to me at all, especially if they drink from the same bottle,' Lotando told him. She received a glimpse from Winster who was playing a game of chess with Jack on the other seat.

Never liked the finality and precision in her words. It was very direct and authentic. 'Your friend was right. It is really hard to analyse Lotando Urey.'

'Oh great, the signpost read 60km from Mutare. I'm so tired,' Chenai stretched out her fingers. They crackled with tension.

'You don't like travelling, do you?' Godfrey asked his voice muffled.

A wet towel rinsed by bottle water covered his face. He felt cooler. He didn't like traveling, but he liked adventures. It was something new to brag about back at college the following term.

'No, I do very much. Maybe that's the reason I chose to come along. I like a little excitement occasionally. Anyway, I couldn't have stayed behind alone with Ashley being here and all. Mostly, I've nothing to do until mid-August,' she explained.

'What will you be enrolling for at var? Got any acceptances yet?'

Chenai gazed out of the window viewing the forests and mountains from afar. 'I'm expecting a reply sometime in July from MU accepting me for Biomedical Sciences. I hope I'll qualify or I'll simply die.'

'Peterhouse groomed you well. Almost all the chicks from there come out clean. With the fellas, that's another story – look at me.' There was a hint of sadness in his voice. 'How many points did you get?'

Chenai shrugged a bit. 'Thirteen.'

'I know what will happen to you, Cheny. You'll receive a reply with something else.'

Chenai was confused. 'What, how do you know?'

'Most of the girls from my first original stream came out with those kind of points and even less. They were given Medicine right away and they happily took it. They are now second or third years, I think.'

Chenai was silent for a moment. She always dreamed of doing Medicine, but the going was always a fourteen or fifteen unless of course you knew someone influential at the institution it was being offered. She had almost cried when she had come out with thirteen points at her Advanced Levels. She could have been happy with less. *Why so close, but yet so far?* She was emotionally offended. She had opted for Biomedicine instead whilst applying at MU. MU was in the top three of the highly rated unis in the country. She hoped

Godfrey wasn't dishonest.

Why would he? 'Are you still doing IT at Speciss?'

'I'm finishing in May,' Godfrey said. 'I hope we'll start together at MU or maybe I'll go to Wits. A degree in Comp Scie would be cool, don't you think? I've chosen to do something with my life. I'm dying for some change,' he added lowly.

Chenai stared at him astound. Unfortunately, she couldn't see his face. *Such words coming from the Horse's mouth, what was the world coming to?*

Winster couldn't afford being beaten again. He had to equal the matches otherwise, he was going to enter the Eastern Highlands disappointed. A draw would be a far better result, he thought. Jack didn't want a draw. He was sixteen, Winster was older, and he was ahead in the game. He needed to show this Urey boy that he was the smartest of them all.

CHAPTER FOURTEEN

Destination Pending

The bus was parked outside a mini-hotel fixed on an en route stop, bus station and all. The place was composed of various vehicles from a huge bus jam-packed with country people to jeeps inhibited by foreign and local tourists wearing summer clothes. The signpost on the side of the road read *TO NYAMAROPA*. Below it, a numeric figure had faded before a *two* then *km* in rusty brown colour.

'Before we begin, we need a prayer to keep us safe on the rest of our journey,' Father Rosina said, positioned in front of the bus. 'Can anybody lead us in prayer? Ms Lotando Urey, please.'

Lot felt slammed. *Why me?* Praying wasn't her specialty by far. She thought of refusing – perhaps give an excuse. *What kind of excuses did one give for evading praying to a crowd?*

Damn, she thought and multi-sec composed a swift prayer. *Oh my, this is sorted.*

'I pray that we do what we came here to do in a safe non-controversial manner and leave safely in the name of Jesus Christ, Amen!'

She heard a giggle and she knew it was either Winster or Brenla. She didn't know what pissed her the most. *Swift and precise and to hell with what you all think about my prayer,* she thought without opening her eyes yet. *I'm here because of a woman called Yana, damn her!*

'Thank you, Ms Urey,' Father Rosina thanked sweetly. 'Where we are heading, unfortunately we can't take the bus with us. We have to use the transport obtainable here. Forests enchant this place and the roads are too narrow. Please can we carry our belongings, as you can see it's near five in the evening, we better get going. I'm sure all of you need rest. It has been a long day.'

Amen, the driver thought. His job was done. His room was waiting. *God Bless the Eastern Highlands and their hospitality,* he praised happily.

'From here, Mr Legondo will be staying at The *VaWasu Lodges* patiently waiting for us on our three-week stay. We'll of course have the medical attention of Dr Mwanza, not to mention that Ms Urey here is also capable.'

A snort came – very rudely audible. Yana leered at Brenla who frowned back.

'Can we move our luggage from this bus now, please?' Father Rosina continued, carrying his own flashy suitcase. The group exited the bus saying polite goodbyes to Mr Legondo.

In a few minutes' time, they were safely seated in green Toyota Hilux Jeeps. The Jeeps had dirty cream leather hoods, carved nettled bunkers and three comfortable broad row-seats each. The first ride held Father Rosina and the medic, with their entire luggage, the mounds of sanitation and foodstuffs affiliated it leaving no room for a third. This meant that the other nine had to occupy the second Toyota. They sat three a seat.

The first seat behind the driver comprised of Yana, Tawanda and Lotando. The second had Brenla, Never and Godfrey whilst the rear sat Chenai, Jack and Winster.

Their driver was a brown, kinky haired man with a wrinkled face and an amazingly lathe body. His mouth formed a thin line and wasn't of a conversational quality. A mouth that maybe spoke twice a day, a mouth that minded its own business.

Lotando tried to close her mind from the presumably silly argument, an argue-whisper according to the level of voice output.

'I didn't have a choice, did I?' Tawanda groaned in contention.

'What is a choice?' Yana, like always, spoke her piece of mind openly. 'Sitting with Bretty was nothing, but a choice!' she made sure that Brenla wouldn't hear her. Anyway, there was no need because the three at their back were loud in conversation.

'This is ridiculous. Lotando, tell her she has got it all very wrong,' Tawanda looked for a way out.

'Eh, Eh, please *ndisiyeyi* in this *nyaya* of yours,' Lot waved her hands in protest.

'Can't you see that she is mad at you as well, Tawa?' Yana emphasized.

'Mad at me because I sat with Brenla?' Tawanda said agitated. '*Imi* girls *imi, munopenga here?*'

Lotando glared at him reproachfully. 'Hey, don't say "you girls", say "you Nana". I said leave me out of this, okay?' she sort of shouted.

This got the attention of the others. Tawanda sulked.

'What's wrong up there?' Jack cried from the rear.

'Mind your own business, young fella,' Yana cried back, not rudely, but firmly.

Jack frowned and left it alone. He pursued his exciting conversation with Chenai.

The Jeep finally sliced into the rough terrain expanded by trees and bushes of various heights and sizes. Although narrow, the roads were practically clearly sufficient to traverse without any obstacles. The road they took went in corners and seemed to be escalating uphill at one time then downhill at other spectrums. As they drove deeper, the mountainous vegetation began to creep up constantly fusing landscapes interconnected with greener grasses and browner trees.

The air suddenly became cooler and the wind increased in intensity.

CHAPTER FIFTEEN

The Chamber

The vehicles circled four times changing courses. The place was already playing host to some of the unknown. Father Rosina vigorously climbed out of the first Jeep and gracefully went to greet their *leader*.

The place looked extra-intricate like nothing they had ever set eyes on. It represented an unfinished dome of stonework missing a crown. It comprised of a series of dry stonewall enclosures inside, which were probably remains of huts and granaries. The site was situated on top of a median high hill and promoted its inhibiters with clear views over the surrounding land. Bushes forming a square a few meters away from the rendezvous thickened the exterior covering. The smooth peaceful sound of a flowing spring could be heard from the other side of the stones.

The building was well carved to accommodate two sets of character. From the East, you entered into the main big arena, that looked more like a court martial vacant. Concealed compartments made part of the different wings. The current setting of the main arena indicated that it had been thoroughly modified and that someone had been using the place not far from that day.

The compartments were made of well-constructed walls that characterized low entrances, small square loopholes and there were parapets on inner sides of the perimeter walls. Father Rosina now stood with the other people. The nine from Harare were particularly stunned to see other people there especially of the same age as they. Nobody had informed them there would be other people there.

There was an older Pastor in a black polo shirt and white collar.

He was probably in his late fifties. His hair was cut short, but adequately available to use a comb. His eyes were brown and sleepy – the kind that would sleep on you anywhere if there was long silence. He was averagely sized in weight and medium in height. He smiled at them and they shook hands. He had with him nine individuals. They looked physically, mentally and socially diversified in numerous terms.

'Gather around, please,' Father Rosina said, gesturing them to merge into a group.

The driver of Lot's Jeep came over and whispered something to his ear. The two drifted and stopped at a distance. He gave him a cellphone. They whispered something to each other for a while. Lot felt something. She was sure they had glanced at her more than once – directly at her.

Why? She thought confused. *Maybe I'm just nervous and seeing stuff.*

Father Rosina pocketed the cellphone, returned and reclaimed his position whilst the drivers left with their Jeeps.

'Permit me to introduce my dear old friend, Reverend Mango of *St Patrick's Anglican Church, Mutare.* To those who don't know me, brothers and sisters, my name is Gama Rosina from the Cathedral Centre, Harare. Take over please, Reverend Mango,' he smiled at him.

'Thank you, Father,' Reverend Mango's voice was lovely to consume. 'Firstly, I'd like to offer one of my own to lead us in prayer before anything else. It is wise to put the Lord upfront.'

'Let us pray,' automatically as if taught to respond instantly to that speech, one of his people began softly. 'Our Father, who art in heaven, thy kingdom come, thy will be done as on Earth as it is in Heaven. Give us this day, our daily bread and forgive us for our trespasses as we forgive those who trespass against us, deliver us from evil for yours is the kingdom, the power, and the glory forever. Father, our God, Our Lord, we would like to take this opportunity to thank You for guiding us on our journeys this Good Friday so as to reach here in peace at Your chosen place without the devil's intervention. Please take care of our beloved new friends and us so that we may spend the following days in happiness and loving civilization. In the name of the Father and the Holy Ghost I pray, may peace be with us all, Amen!' Other Amens concurred.

They all opened their eyes. Lotando felt like clapping.

That was one good prayer. One jolly good one, she thought, looking at the prayer.

'Thank you, Ms Kezi,' Father Mango bowed slightly. 'On this good Good Friday, I'd like to greet you, Father Rosina, and your youths in the Name of Jesus. We may all be aware that we are gathered here to gather knowledge about the life of our Lord who looks upon us daily as His lambs. I'd like to thank and compliment all of you in agreeing to leave your comfortable homes in sacrifice to come to this open and remote place to share your gifted thoughts,' Father Mango said and paused. His speech publicized years of experience and matureness in addressing a crowd of any sort. His voice was soft, but all of them heard it despite the wind's fluctuating velocities.

However, he continued. 'Father Rosina and company, permit me to introduce my youths. Please come aside as I call your name. Mr Pondai Mhara.'

A chap about the age of twenty-three came out from the crew and stood a couple of meters away. He had long black thin dreadlocks. His eyes were of a light brown distinctive colour. He wasn't that tall, but his body had matured well. He was a sturdy individual who walked and scrutinized his surroundings with flexibility. He looked fearless and he looked money for his clothes said so.

'Thank you. Mr Daniel Gota.'

This one looks simple, Lotando thought. *He must be one of the unfortunate ones, probably an orphan.* He looked young, about twenty or less. His hair was short and his eyes looked very ambitious. However, his mouth looked less talkative and, as Lot looked on, their eyes seemed to cross paths. He was definitely shy for he looked away instantly, blushing at first then turning grave like the weather. Somehow, Lotando couldn't help noticing that beneath all that gloom, he really looked more than okay. A glance at Brenla made that official. Brenla was just attracted. The guy stood next to Mr Mhara.

'Thank you. Ms Shamiso Dube.'

To Tawanda's scrutiny, this was a stunner. She was very light in complexion and her eyes were brown diamonds. She wore a model's smile as she swayed aside. It was beyond doubt that she came from a well-established family, with lots of money to spare on silk jeans and two hundred dollars athletic shoes. To Lotando she was the mirror of Brenla, but her friendly facial features and air suggested lots.

'Thank you. Mr Ishmael Loudha.'

He was definitely Indian, and he looked all *wolfy*. This made him look older than even Father Rosina did, but Yana figured out that he was probably eighteen or nineteen. He was taller than nineteen, but his blue sparkling eyes were of a one year old. He looked wealthy from the colour of his visible skin and body weight, but his clothes were simple. He was calm as a still sea at night. He joined his group.

'Thank you. Ms Diana Kezi.'

It was hard to place this lady. Her complexion was a bit low in the light part. Her eyes were brown. She was averagely built with a great symmetrical body. The chaps from Harare couldn't help staring at her. She was somewhere around the twenty-fifth year mark. Despite her lovely appearance, she looked dull in spirit much to Never's disappointment. Never couldn't believe this was the individual who had prayed for them minutes ago. Firstly, she was too damn sexy to be considered as a church lady and her face was too sad to be considered as a lady of the church.

Why so dark, Never thought, *and yet so light?*

'Thank you. Ms Colodia Munyaradzi.'

As sharp as she looked was as sharp as she reacted. She wore spectacles, her curiously long hair pinned backwards and her complexion was Lotando light. She looked intellectually gifted in any way and very beautiful. The Harare sons couldn't help feeling lucky that all the new ladies looked breathtakingly delicate. Colodia was just the same height as Lotando. Her social identity was possibly moderate, but once again, Lotando's gifted eye saw that she was one of the unfortunate ones – in some way. Yana could also tell. She could distinguish some not yet-fully healed covered-up bruises on her face. There was no denying the causes. She felt sorry for the young lady who looked very much a freshman.

'Thank you. Mr Tawanda Sisoko.'

Tawanda *part 2* was a twenty-three-year-old coloured and he looked to be one poor soul. His clothes didn't even match his description. All the Harare ladies – Brenla upfront – were instantaneously indoctrinated by his mixed looks. He had that ginger kind of hair that was well placed on his scalp. It looked like it hadn't been washed for days. His eyes were marvellously brown, fusing with his light brown complexion. His height was just perfect, and his body looked moderately fit. Yana could discern some previous diseases attacking it, and possible bad habits paining it. Tawanda *part 1* was amused by the idea of having a *sazita* around. He knew he was going to be Ash from then on.

'Thank you. Mr Ignatius and Mr Ian Mvuu.'

The twins looked Winster's age, very troublesome and as mischievous as they looked alike. It was distinguishable that the two came from a huge country family somewhere very rural. They wore out dated, but representable clothes. They looked as thin as they were tall. Their hair must have taken lots of effort to comb because it looked like masses of wire brush. Lotando and Chenai resisted the urge to laugh. The two looked very funny and adorable. The twins made funny salutes at Father Mango as they drifted to their group. Father Mango suppressed a laugh.

'Thank you, thank you very much,' Father Mango concluded.

The two groups of nines had been separated as it was at first. Father Rosina wasted no time in introducing his own. After that, they all exchanged handshakes and pleasantries.

As Lotando had estimated, the twins had a lot to offer than handshakes. To her astonishment, their English was far better than Ishmael's was, even better than Yana's – basically because their grammar was polite and no swearing word appeared in their vocabulary.

The two priests gave them a swift tour of the place. They were showed to their different quarters. The ladies were to camp at the west compartment where less wind was available as in noise and the gentlemen at the southern side on steeper slope. They were all impressed by the designs the compartments had been modified with to be habitable and comfortable. It seemed like the entire place was colourful, with many flower plants including marigolds, West Indian Lemongrass, Mother-in-Law's Tongue and small cinnamon trees. The priests took a smaller compartment to share with the medic on the northern side. After they arranged their belongings in their new residences, they gathered at the main seminar arena.

Six powerful solar-battery lamps and a small fire in the middle lighted up the place. The medical assistant and Father Rosina were brewing a huge pot of tea flanked by a pot of peeled potatoes and baked beans using a huge charcoal stove-like stand at the far side.

The ladies went over to assist with the eats. As they couldn't all help, only four were permitted to assist by Father Rosina. *Likewise,* Lotando fumed as she watched Brenla happily stay behind. Brenla had suddenly become the centre of attraction to the other girls from Mutare as she gave them a good *Brenla Hewstone Outline* of what a dreamland place Harare was and what she did for a living.

Lot, Yana, Chenai and Diana had chosen to dodge this intimidating phase and had happily passed on the plates to the chaps who sat happily at one corner discussing guys' stuff. The fireplace was constructed with four surrounding arching stone-benches at about a five-meter radius from the focus. The campers sat six on each bench and the last was reserved for the priests and Derrick. After dinner, Father Mango gave his speech.

'I'd like to thank you all once again for choosing to come here at your own will. Officially, our camping rationale begins on Monday. Therefore, as it is now Friday, we will take tomorrow and Sunday to get familiar with each other and the place.

'It is always wise to begin early, so I'll give you a brief outline of how we are going to be living in the next three weeks. For a start, I'll give you a background of where we are for knowledge's sake. We are in the forestlands of *Inyanga* – in the mountains. This area is christened by the *Inyangombe River.* Although Stone Age and early Iron Age sites are less evident than those of the late Iron Age, the late Iron Age period at Inyanga was typified by features such as terraces, pathways and by stone walls of uncovered, undressed masonry that favoured structures such as pits, huts and forts. Speaking about forts, this settlement we currently inhabit was called *Fort Uda.* The early settlers, mainly Portuguese traders that had crossed the Mozambican border in the colonial era, used it many years back. They are presumed to have vehemently raided an undefined clan to settle here wishing to ward off animal attacks and other oppressions. They never really found it comfortable here because it was a weakly designed fort with numerous incursion holes. They called it *The Torture Chamber.* Modern Historians claim that this place was mainly called that because of the unrest, presumably believed to be a result of curses cast upon the Torture Chamber by the prior settlers in retaliation.

'Anyway, that was never proven – it's an old exaggerated tale. No need to worry about spirits. Many have been here before and no such things have been identified. The last two decades have proven that, that is, since it was explored. The Torture Chamber is situated about twelve kilometres from the main road to *Nayamaropa*, which divides this area with the *Nyanga National Park*. On the way, you may pass along the *Nyangombe Falls*, which is a nice attraction to watch considering the last time I was here. A few kilometres southwest is a farm. There is a clear road that leads there, many roads lead there actually, many being shortcuts. If we stick together and don't wander off unnoticed, we'll be okay. I assume that that won't be a problem. Father Rosina?'

Father Rosina belched silently and cleared his throat. 'Excuse me – thank you, Father Mango. I'll take over from there.'

The others stared at the fading fire. The sky was now dark and cooler. The moon was halfway up and the stars were starting to glitter the sky.

CHAPTER SIXTEEN

Authority and Classification

The eighteen looked over at Father Rosina who was going over a small pad book. He flipped over a few pages, and then smiled. He looked satisfied.

'Ladies and gentlemen,' he began, 'as you are all aware, we are here to learn about the wonderful Word of God. In order to learn from others you need to find out what the others think. This is why Father Mango and I have devised a system to have all of us heard. You're going to split into three groups – meaning six for each. In accordance, you are going to be mixed, three from each sector. The arrangement is going to be like; the first group is going to be composed of Ms Chenai Muchemwa, Ms Brenla Hewstone, Mr Never Dotona, Ms Diana Kezi, Mr Ishmael Loudha and Mr Tawanda Sisoko. Please can you rearrange, the first group sits over there,' Father Rosina called out and the first six sat on the first bench. The others stood up.

'The next group, Ms Yana Urey, Mr Winster Urey, Mr Jack Dotona, Ms Colodia Munyaradzi, Ms Shamiso Dube and Mr Pondai Mhara,' Father Rosina called out.

The second group sat accordingly. The last group was evidently clear, but he called them out anyway.

'The last group, Ms Lotando Urey, Mr Tawanda Muchemwa, Mr Godfrey Hewstone, Mr Ian and Mr Ignatius Mvuu and lastly Mr Daniel Gota.'

Father Rosina stood up and looked down on them. Father Mango did the same.

'These are going to be your groups for the following weeks. You'll work as teams. Every team has a leader and I'm proud to say that a few of you previously volunteered, rather volunteered willingly when you signed your papers,' Father Rosina smiled at them.

Lotando knew what was coming and was eager to witness the effects.

'With due consideration and careful scrutiny,' Father Mango took over. 'We have chosen the following people to be your leaders. The first group will be led by,' he took a brief look in Father Rosina's small pad book. 'Ah, Ms Brenla Hewstone.'

Brenla shrieked in delight much to the Urey ladies annoyance. *CEO everywhere, that sucks,* they thought.

'The next group will be headed by Ms Yana Urey.'

Lotando made sure she saw a clean close-up of Yana's face in the light provided by the lamplights. She was gratified. She wished she had a camera. Yana was shocked beyond comparison. Winster gave Yana a congratulations' pat on the back. Amazingly, Shamiso and Colodia gave her delightful congratulations. Yana was too stunned to answer or even blink.

'The remaining group will be the responsibility of Mr Daniel Gota.'

The twins shouted out friendly boos. 'We thought all leaders were women here, Father,' Ignatius cried out. Laughter filled the air.

'Why was our special lady not chosen?' Ian crooned.

Lotando blushed. She was the only female member in her group – she felt overprotected and funny.

Father Rosina and Father Mango exchanged grins.

'Your special lady didn't want to be a leader. Father Rosina said that she made that point pretty clear when she signed her forms,' Father Mango explained.

'Father, you mean to say that if I had signed *yes* on the *want to be a team leader* column on the forms we signed to be here, I could have been chosen?' Ishmael was amazed. His accent was mildly Indian. The Harare ladies liked his accent. It always sounded as if the guy was singing in between his words.

'Yes, Mr Loudha,' Father Rosina replied. 'That was all you had to do, just a tick of ink to win yourself authority.'

'But, but...' Yana began confused. 'But I didn't sign anything saying, *"want to be a team leader."'*

Lotando hid behind the shadows. *Sweet revenge, Nana, got you, you prick.*

'You are saying you don't remember signing your papers on the *want to be a team leader* box?' Ishmael asked confused as well.

'Yes, I didn't, and –' she said and then stopped. 'I wasn't the one who signed those papers,' she claimed, looking in Lotando's direction. Lot giggled hiding her face in the lamp shadows.

'I thought you wanted to be a leader, you always want to,' Lotando held defensively.

'We'll have our talk later, dear sister,' Yana threatened. Ash and the twins laughed themselves off.

'I'd really love to hear that talk too,' Ian added. The others laughed.

Shamiso cut them short. 'Fathers – may I, please?'

'Please go ahead, Ms Dube.'

'All this leadership and group organization, what exactly is its main purpose?' she asked curiously.

The others stared back at the priests, really wanting to know. They were curious about this sudden arrangement.

'Good question, Ms Dube,' Father Mango noted. 'We're going to have an imitation of a debate seminar so as to speak. You're going to be asked to pick a particular topic or group support topic to defend and offer knowledge on. The grouping arrangement is also meant to make your movements easier and organized during your brief hiking in the mountains, sightseeing.' Murmurs filled the air. This was something new. 'I knew you'd love mountaineering,' Father Mango laughed. 'But back to the group support topics, there are three topics to go on. Firstly, a group will be affirm on *Religion* mainly *Christianity*. The other will base on *Culture and Ethics* whilst the last deals with *Scientific Beliefs and Theories*. Now you are to discuss these topics and debate on what you think about the other topics as compared to yours. Father Rosina, Dr Mwanza and I will be the judges to these debates and pick a winner at the end of the debates. Please choose your topics carefully to avoid future frustration, disappointment and disorganization. We will give you until Sunday to choose. Now, I think all of you need your sleep as much as I do.'

Yana threw Lotando the flip-flops she had packed for her amongst her own things, as they couldn't fit into Lotando's small bags. 'Thanks, Lot, lots of thanks, thanks a lot.'

The girls were preparing to go to sleep in their chamber. Only

Lotando and Yana were still arranging their stuff in the cubicles corner that had been reserved for luggage. The air had a different scent, coming from automatic bottle sprays that were fixed on the walls producing a fragrance that was repellent to crawling things like snakes or lizards. The same kind of sprays were all over the Torture Chamber's structure, but differed in smell with each area from cinnamon, cloves, lime and garlic. This kind of odour was more feminine defined, distinguishing it as the chamber for the ladies. Only Diana was asleep by now.

The others stared at them giggling. They were comfortably snuggled in their huge sleeping bags gracefully provided by the church courtesy of sponsorship from Mutare University. Each bag was so huge to capacitate two people and they felt extremely comfortable in them.

'Group leader? What a mess I am in,' Yana blustered. 'Thanks a lot.'

'You are welcome,' Lotando replied grinning. 'You are welcome, Yana.'

'How could you do this to me, Lot? You little devil.'

Lotando glowered at her. 'Hey, what kind of devil firstly forged my signature to get me here without my approval or knowledge? Tell me, kind old angel.'

Yana looked guilty, sulking. She inserted herself into her sleeping bag and frowned at her. 'Damn you.'

'Damn you too, bug off!'

'You know what? I'd like to kick your little ass numb if the others were asleep,' Yana groaned.

'I wouldn't have loved to do anything other than that to yours, snitch,' Lotando retorted. She strolled to her sleeping bag and cocooned in.

'Oh, boy, you girls are good!' Colodia laughed. 'You are so tight.'

'Couldn't get tighter,' Brenla grimaced looking sideways. 'Or crazier,' she added in a whisper.

'Not you, Brenla,' Yana had owl ears. 'Not now, please.'

Brenla wisely didn't respond. She fell asleep grinning.

By that time, the chaps were busy snoring in their quarters exhausted from their long journey.

CHAPTER SEVENTEEN

Religious Reign

The campers spent most of Saturday sightseeing in their designated groups, discussing on what kind of topic to choose. The priests and Derrick chose to go to the nearby spring to collect buckets of sanitation water to store in their onsite secure aluminium camping tanks.

Drinking water was being provided by a borehole that was built at the Chamber plus the mineral water bottles they had brought from their towns. The eighteen were forbidden to help. Instead, they were chased away to enjoy themselves in the woods.

The region was partly of dry savannah woodland and forest. All in some, the altitude was estimated to be around 1 878m above sea level receiving rainfall amounting to 970mm. The hottest month recorded had been that reaching a low 37°C and the coldest month 11°C. The population was about 2 900 people.

As the youths enjoyed the scenery, they followed terraces subsequent to the contours of the hill, which were often interrupted by steep and narrow stone built paths, or wide unpaved roadways that tended to diagonally cut through them. Clearly, no signs of notable wildlife existed though different types of birds could be seen flying by. As suggested, they only circled the area around the Torture Chamber, frequently relaxing on big weathered boulders made of granite rock.

On Sunday, it was all mayhem by midday. They had been compelled to a long Easter Sunday sermon by Father Mango. The sermon had begun from nine in the morning up to eleven. To Lotando, they were the worst two hours for her that year. It was exactly three years since she had attended a church service and it hadn't felt any better. The selection of the chosen topics was to be heard at three in the afternoon after brief discussions.

It was now ten minutes after three and they were sitting in the main chamber. Momentarily, they were gathered at a spot designed to hold conferences or stage acts. It had a beautifully designed stage with a reading stand carved of solid rock. Behind it was a stone bench that could accommodate twelve averagely sized people. Father Rosina and Derrick sat there waiting. Father Mango stood behind the stomach-level rock stand, his Bible resting peacefully on top.

The eighteen sat below, looking up at him with eager eyes. They sat on three stone benches reserved for the crowd. They could have sat anywhere in the limit of six benches, but they had chosen to occupy the first three sitting according to their groups. The environment was currently at instability.

'Please, please,' Father Mango cried out. 'Please let us settle down and see what we can do to solve this matter.'

Brenla's group sat upfront, followed by Yana's, reared by Lotando's.

'We seem to be having disparities on choices. It seems like most of you want to be given the Religion topic and that leaves us in a dilemma of identity. However, for it to be fair, Father Rosina and I have decided to play lotto with you.'

'We got ours,' Ian quipped. 'We don't need extra.'

The others giggled. Lotando felt funny. The twins liked her a lot, and they had become her favourite people at the camp so far.

'Father Rosina and I have labelled three similar sized cards with a topic. What we will do is we will put these cards into this empty container. Your leader is required to come up stage and dip their hand into it and, without looking, pick one. That will automatically be your topic – no turning back. Ms Hewstone, please come up stage and begin the procedure,' Father Mango suggested, receiving the selected plastic container from Derrick.

Brenla climbed up the stage and directly went for the container without hesitation or sign of anxiety. 'May I?'

Father Mango nodded smiling. She dipped her hand in and raised it almost instantaneously holding her topic. She gave it to Father Mango without looking. Father Mango looked at it and smiled broadly.

'Ms Hewstone and her group will be for Religion.'

Brenla's bench erupted with joy. The others groaned in agony.

I wasted my time jotting down those NIV notes for nothing, Lotando thought furiously.

'Next up,' Father Mango said. 'Ms Urey.'

Yana shrugged and went up stage. She hesitated for a while, looking down at Brenla who was grinning at her. *Damn your sticky fingers,* Yana wanted to say, but managed to limit it as a thought. She dipped for her topic and, like Brenla, gave it to Father Mango without looking. Father Mango smiled once more. Yana was already halfway down to her seat when it was announced. She didn't expect anything good after Brenla's mammoth luck. She had spent most of her time browsing the Bible for nothing and nothing changed the fact that it was possibly for nothing.

'Ms Urey and her group will be for Science,' Father Mango announced.

This time Lotando groaned as well. That was it; she was kicked in the ass. Her counterparts wriggled uncomfortably whilst Winster and Jack sighed with relief and somewhat joy. Colodia couldn't hide her excitement. She patted Yana on the back and became the first person besides the Harare crew to call her Doc.

'That means we will be for Culture,' Daniel supposed without standing up to finish the draw. There was no need.

'That is true, Mr Gota,' Father Mango concurred extracting the last card and suspended the container upside down for them to see that the draw hadn't been rigged. He held the last card above for them all to see. It was written *CULTURE* in bold. 'Now that that is settled, we now know our responsibilities. You are required to say something about your topics for starters. What it is good for *humanity*, its benefits to us or such. The first presentations will basically be intros to show your knowledge on the topic. This task is expected to be carried out by the group leaders. Along time, as we go on with our seminar, a group can choose its speakers independently. The presentation schedule will go like this. Tomorrow, we'll begin with Religion. On Wednesday, it will be Science, then on Friday, Culture. Thank you all for understanding, ladies and gentleman.'

Monday, 10:47A.M.

'Christianity is the doctrine of Christian faith, a Christian religious system of faith, conduct and characters of the Christendom. Christianity has grown to be the largest of all religions. By definition, Christians are the followers of Jesus Christ, the Son of God. Christianity makes us celebrate Holy days such as Advent, Christmas, Palm Sunday, Good Friday and yesterday – Easter Sunday. There are many divisions within Christianity. The most prominent being Protestantism, the Roman Catholic Church, the Easter Orthodox Church – and Mormonism from the Church of Jesus Christ Latter Day Saints found in 1830 by Joseph Smith. Each has its own way of worshipping, but despite their differences, all Christian groups share a belief in the teachings of Jesus. Most Christians worship by meetings in groups called congregations. They pray together and sing sacred songs called hymns. Today, more than 1 600 million people throughout the world practice Christianity. Christians believe it is their duty to help alleviate the suffering of the poor and sick. Christianity is a broad subject that requires careful thought and insight. It is after all the Grand of all Religions. My group and I rest our giving here, thank you,' Brenla finished with due pomp. She stepped off the stage whilst the others clapped.

Lotando was too consumed to believe her ears. She didn't believe she had just heard one of the smoothest speeches coming from *Bretty*.

It must have been the fusion of enormous teamwork, she thought not convinced. However, as she thought about it further, she couldn't get Brenla's picture when she had presented her topic. Her eye contact, air, posture and all had been purely superb like a confident CEO presenting a doubtful budget to the Board of Directors. For once, she respected Brenla for that. Her CEO trend at her father's company had groomed her well.

Wednesday, 11:16 A.M.

'Life and our topic are correlated. One can't live without the other. Science, ladies and gentleman, is the knowledge of facts obtained by careful study. It is a branch of knowledge dealing with numerous areas such as the nature of matter, natural forces, us humans, etcetera. Space travel, computers and reliable medical care are just a few of the things that owe their existence to Science. Two hundred and fifty years ago, most people lived no longer than thirty-five years. Today, in the industrialized parts of the world, the average life span has increased to more than seventy years. This is because of the development of Science. The world is moving much faster than anything because of Science and because of those who study Science, these being the Scientists and the Philosophers of the world. Science is an extremely huge subject to discuss or define and nobody can hope to know it all. My own and I will leave it here for now. Thank you,' Yana stepped down from the stage. The spectators applauded.

Lotando felt proud. *Spoken like a true scientist,* she thought. Somehow, she couldn't help feeling jealous for not being chosen in the same group. She too was going to be a scientist and tackling such a subject would have been a stroll in the park and fun.

No deceit, she knew that the others knew that her group's topic was one hell of a trying glitch.

Friday, 11:30 A.M.

'Our topic, Culture, tells us about our origin. It tells us about the manners and customs of people. Different or not, where we are going and where we are coming from is our culture. We rest our case for now. Thank you.'

Simple and brief and the applause couldn't have been louder. As Daniel stepped down from the stage superseded by Father Rosina, he couldn't have looked more satisfied. Yana gazed back at Lot sitting on the third bench and grinned. Lotando knew she didn't need to have looked back to check for she already knew.

The speech had been so swift, direct and effective – not wasting time or space on anything semantic. It was so *Lotish.*

Lotando smiled back at her. *What did you want me to do?* She thought. *Nobody had a bloody idea of how we were going to start. I just said out a few words.*

In fact, those few words had turned out to be exactly the speech. She hadn't known anyone with a carbon copy memory such as Daniel.

'Thank you,' Father Rosina stood behind the stand. 'Thank you for your admirable presentations. I'm pleased to say that I am proud that you are getting along to be able to put your heads together. Your coordination so far for the first week here has been filled with love and expanded your understanding of each other.

The Lord is indeed looking after us all. We are safe, my friends. I hope we'll keep our faith in the Lord and continue our happy stay here. Let us please bow for a short prayer.'

They all bowed and Father Rosina let out a brief prayer. Moments later, the guys went around the place, watering the flowers, which they had been informed were mainly planted around as snake repellents and needed maintenance. Afterwards, they were sitting somewhere in the woods, enjoying the sunshine whilst playing a game of cards provided by the classy Ash. The ladies found it fitting to do their washing and help each other do their hairs. The priests and the medic were busy drinking hot chocolate, whilst exchanging some views on the current burning issues on politics. It was all good at the Torture Chamber.

CHAPTER EIGHTEEN

Flag Combinations

The groups took turns of threes to have baths at a well-reserved screened-off sanitation area on the edge of the Chamber. The bathing quarters were situated at the east wing close to a niche spring that provided adequate water for both occasions. Their waste disposal facilities were three toilets smartly built at the far area of that east wing. It was practically deserted and sometimes hard to locate if you were somehow new to the place. The days passed in discovering the Chamber's familiar territories, Sunday number two being a day of further exploration. The group from Harare and the Mutare group swiftly adapted to each other much to the priests' joy. They were calling each other on the nickname basis.

They woke up on Sunday a very tired entity. The twins were unusually quiet. They weren't themselves as of late. Moments of jokes came, but differed away rather abruptly. Lotando couldn't help noticing that her admirers somehow looked sick. They frequently visited the east wing side more than often. The others barely noticed it because the twins were by now famous for their awesome appetites, which hadn't faltered. Lotando couldn't help noticing that Tawanda didn't look so good as well.

She had slighted the thoughts off as possible anxiety or stomach problems. It was on Tuesday when they had to present their topic's authenticity and defend it against the other groups resourced of twelve bright individuals.

Lot's group had a hard time trying to formulate a strategy. Automatically, they had turned to her, and she had refused to be their spokesperson. Ash was voted for that task and he had given in reluctantly.

Yana and her group had many ideas. Yana had designated Winster as their spokesperson. That issue was a debate to all, but in the end, nobody wanted to take on the wrath of Religion and Culture. They needed someone who had a sharp responsive mind. Yana knew whom to pick and chose him. It had taken Jack and the other girls to persuade *little Einstein* to agree. He had no choice. But then, in the end, after careful consideration and a few intense new debates, Winster had won. His leader had compromised.

Their Saturday night had passed in formulating answers and counter answers. Amazingly, Pondai, who they had discovered to be a Civil Engineer by profession, had programmed their details with state oriented approach. They were confident that their first time affirming their topic was going to be flawless.

That Sunday's service appeared to have been shorter in comparison to the prior. Lotando and many had figured it was their anxiety to begin the debates. Some thought it was because Father Rosina had led the service. He had a youthful approach towards his preaching, and they had enjoyed it. His main discourse had been about abstaining from early sex and being faithful to each other.

At three in the afternoon, cloud cover had enveloped the Chamber and the surrounding forest looked dark and foreign. The groups were ready for the first genuine debate.

'Now, now,' Father Rosina cried out. 'Let's settle. We are about to begin. The first group will offer its case whilst the rest listens. If there are any questions, they will have to be asked after that. Ms Hewstone and company, may you please own the stage.'

As if to make it more intriguing, Brenla and her crew held Bibles, small notepads and pencils as they went upstage. As expected, Brenla took the stand and placed her Bible on top. Chenai, Diana, Ishmael, Tawanda and Never squeezed themselves onto the stage's bench.

Father Rosina, Father Mango and Derrick sat behind the two spectating groups on the fourth bench leaving the third bench to work as a table for them. They had their own Bibles, jotting pads and pencils there.

Brenla cleared her throat and began.

'My colleagues and I would like to restore and prove that our topic is indeed the basis of humanity. This has been proved in many circumstances over the last two thousand years. Initially, for us to understand the meaning of Christianity we must circumspectly look at its origin. Its origin is none other than the Son of the Creator, our Almighty God. Jesus Christ was sent down to Earth leaving His place with the Father in Heaven to resolve the "was eroding humanity". Evil had conquered the world and because of Christ, evil was mitigated and humanity was given hope. Christ forgave sinners, fed many, healed, and gave life to the dead. His powers were and are still matched by none. His attitude and constitution encouraged the emergence of life and peace in the world that we live today. By so doing, He sacrificed His life for us all when He died on the cross. People killed the Son of God, but people were saved and forgiven. There may be some religions out there that do not believe in Christianity, but may I ask why they do believe in God. Cultures try to hide and deceive people about Christ, Science tries to open our eyes to God's extraordinary creations, and yet we believe in Science now as in God, but not in Christ.

So many people in this world are dreadfully ignorant. They claim *life is what it is not what it is claimed to be*. Would we still be living in this world if it weren't because of Christianity? Would Christmas, Easter, and other special Christian occasions exist if it weren't because of Christianity? People claim Christianity to be a biased fairy tale, but why do they celebrate Christmas, why do they love each other on the festive seasons and exchange gifts? I believe in *where we are going and where we are coming from*, but simplicity in tacit datum tells us *where you go is where you are going to end up at, not where you are coming from*. Cultural and Spiritual practices existed. Jesus came along, things changed.

Would there be some peace in the world if it weren't because of Christianity, its followers and believers? I think not. Science would exist, but by now, we would possibly be the substrate outputs of nuclear wars. Culture would have still existed, but we'd still be living in caves, in the days of human suppression. Africa would be a worse place to live. *What is life without Christianity, but no life?'*

Brenla stopped, letting the question hang out in perpetual limbo. Whether true or false, positive or negative, the words had killed a fly and kissed the sting of a bee.

'We stop for now. Any questions?'

Everybody started to shout his or her questions in disarray at her. She glared at them blank.

'I could do with some hand raising to save time,' she grimaced.

The twelve below glared at her amused. *Now what are we, your pupils?* Lotando thought offended. *I bet my hand will be invisible to you sister.*

Realizing her graveness to be pure, hands shot up. Brenla took her time in choosing, frustrating Yana.

'Hmm, Shamiso.'

'Thank you,' Shamiso said. 'I'd like to know something, don't Christians use Science?'

'They do, and?'

'Science and Christianity both encourage the existence and prosperity of humanity, don't they?'

'Yes, they do,' Brenla replied calmly.

'So why did you claim that Christianity is the only true basis of humanity, Brenla?' Shamiso quizzed her.

'I claimed that Christianity is the major base of humanity – the quality of being humane. Science can't work without humanity, which is created by Christianity for it to be,' Brenla emphasized. 'Meaning Christianity is the major basis of humanity. Have I answered your question, Shamie?'

Not at all, Shamiso hesitated, but of course, she knew what the outcome would only be if she tried to argue, so she let it be. She nodded in reply. Hands shot up instantaneously.

Brenla grinned. 'Tawanda – Ash.'

'Thanks,' Ash smiled. 'Isn't Christianity as biased as you claimed most people say?'

Brenla was taken aback. 'I don't understand.'

'I think you do,' Ash smiled back at her expression. 'Why are there different religions, for example Hinduism, Judaism and so on? Why is it we now have a situation where prophet this, prophetess that suddenly tend to exist every week, miracle moneys, many unexplainable things? The majority of these prophets being from Christianity.'

Brenla looked back at her crew and gestured Ishmael to the stand. Ishmael stood up and took the stand beside Brenla in confidence. '

Some people don't believe in Christ as they do in Muhammad, Buddha and the others. We do, which is why we are supporting Religion as in Christianity. They don't believe that Jesus was the Son of God. They say he was a mortal being just like us, Mohammed and many other prophets who lived to be supreme models. We believe that Jesus is the Son of God and there is no bias in that. Whatever one does, whether they are real prophets, prophetesses or not, Christianity can't be held accountable for atypical human acts.'

Ash nodded, but he wasn't done. 'Is Jesus truly the Son of God?'

Ishmael stared back at him and responded with genuine eyes. 'Yes, he is.'

'Thank you, I'm satisfied, Brenla,' Ash gave it no further go.

Hands shot up. Brenla retained her position as Ishmael returned to sit.

'Er – Winster,' she chose him before his sister. Yana breathed heavily.

'Thanks. Now you said Christianity encourages peace and tranquillity. In other words it is as *pure white like a dove.*'

Brenla smiled down at him. *Easy as I thought,* she mused. 'Yes.'

'Do you have any knowledge on the history of the Roman Catholics?' Winster asked.

Brenla didn't know how to take this. She thought for a moment and gestured Chenai to take stand. Lotando and Yana took that as a major offence. It was a fraudulent tactic.

Chenai took the stand and smiled at Winster. 'We know something,' she crooned.

The Urey ladies and some others thought Winster would simply melt at the sight of Chenai. They groaned inwardly and furiously.

'Does that *something* tell you about how many people were burnt, women as a matter of fact – and even young girls as yourself, were burnt to death early centuries back being accused of being witches by these Christian Churches, basically because these churches didn't understand methods of Science?' Winster asked.

'In a way, it shows some points,' Chenai answered uncomfortably.

'What kind of religion is the Roman Catholic?' Winster asked as if curious. 'I'm sorry, I'm a scientist, I don't know for sure.'

A few giggles came. *That's it brother,* Yana thought pleased, *blow your sweetheart to candy.*

'Roman Catholic is a division of Christianity,' Chenai replied downcast. *I'll get you back for this boy.*

Brenla looked as much disappointed. The first bomb had sneaked through her fort.

'Thank you, Brenla, that's all,' Winster completed with a smile. The other two groups smiled cheerfully.

Brenla repositioned herself at the stand. 'Any more questions?' she asked feebly.

Satisfied, the others kept their hands down, except for one and Brenla had no choice, but to pick it.

'Lotando,' Brenla let out a slight sigh.

'Thank you, Brenla. How does Christianity cohere with humanity?' Lotando asked staring directly into her eyes.

Brenla sighed, *So far so polite.* 'By following in Christ's good path, we'll live a better life. If all of us did so, Earth would be like a pre-heaven.'

'But not all of us do?'

'Yes, not all of us do,' Brenla stared at her curiously. *What powder are you throwing at me?*

'Because not all of us see the benefits of Christ's Way, a.k.a Christianity?'

'Yes.'

Lotando sighed. 'Thank you, Brenla, that's all.'

Brenla glared back at her stunned. *That's all? That's very much unlike you.* She looked down on them confused. Nobody had any more questions.

Yana smiled. Lotando liked to leave you guessing.

That night during dinner, the Christian group were just too Christian to sit alone as a group. The others followed suite. The priests sat with the medic having another political science debate.

'You got one hell of a smart cousin, Otto,' Ian complemented. He was gazing down at the food in his plate, appetite forgotten.

Lotando looked at him smiling. The smile faded as she saw Ignatius not eating as well. The twins looked as dark as ever, and even scraggier. By now, if they were their normal selves they would have been reaping a third meal according to their standards.

'Are you all right, Ian?' Lotando asked concerned.

'What has suddenly happened to you two?' Ash came over from washing his plate. To his standards, one meal was enough. He preferred hot chocolate for dessert and this he could do with seconds anytime.

'*Pas d'appétit*,' Ian replied in a French accent.

'*Je suis plein*,' Ignatius added. Lotando and the others laughed.

'I didn't know country people spoke French,' Godfrey alleged amused.

'We live in Mutare and it's not a country, man. Many foreign visitors love our place. Some come from DRC, Angola, Mozambique, some many more places you know,' Daniel informed them. 'These fellas spent their young lives working at a farm close to the border charming tourists.'

'Thanks for gossiping, Brother Daniel,' Ian grimaced.

Lotando laughed. She could imagine the picture of the two skinnies directing herds of cattle. It was really funny.

'Don't laugh, Lotto,' Ignatius groaned. 'Your laugh makes me want to cry like I'm lost in a grotto.'

Laughter filled their corner as seriousness flanked Brenla's corner. Yana's corner was all science and goose bumps. They knew that tomorrow at ten in the morning they were going to face a wounded Christian lion and a deadly inconspicuous chameleon of Culture.

CHAPTER NINETEEN

Decision Virtues

'If a customer has placed an order which exceeds his credit limit, they send the order to the credit department. However, the order should always be accepted if this is one of your special customers. Science and Religion follow similar traits. If Religion placed an order to Science to help humanity survive, then it's a special customer. A special customer can never live without a special seller. Therefore, Christianity and Science are interrelated. It would be a sin in knowledge to deny this fact. But then, to a further degree, Science can live without Christianity, but not the opposite. This, brothers and sisters, makes Science the basis of humanity more than Christianity and our Cultures and Ethics,' Yana introduced.

Her hair was now braided and she looked like a fierce comic book character on the stand.

'Culture and Science are in a variety of ways two totally diversified effects as much as they tend to come from within each other. Giving a hurried approach to Science as a whole will clearly define its complete dominance towards humanity. Giving a broader approach would only be unfair. Would Christianity or Culture have eradicated many diseases? Would Christianity have invented penicillin? Would lifesaving surgery have been discovered and learned through Culture or Christianity? I think we all know the answer. Brothers and sisters, no Christianity or Culture invented the aeroplane. No Christianity or Culture invented the computer, no Culture or Christianity created the internet. No Culture or Christianity has saved more lives and restored worldwide peace than Science. The degree of errors, incompleteness, contradictions or redundancies including major bias, are all associated with every religion and a whole lot of cultural beliefs. No science is that blemished with doubts. Science proves facts, specifies truth. Religion devastatingly hides vital facts. It creates divisions, wars. It makes people believe in what they don't know or haven't seen. It makes people guess, makes people believe in fixed fate whilst it can be changed. More so, Culture neglects modernization, is an ignorant ministry that envies change whilst it lives and survives on change brought by Science.

People now know more things about themselves and their surroundings, are able to preserve and extend lifespans all because of Science. Many ignorant people refuse to glean lessons from Science because Religion forbids, Culture forbids. *Without knowledge of how to cook a frog, one would sulk and die of hunger whilst living near a river crammed with them. Science is humanity. Humanity is science.* I thank you all for listening,' Yana finished and took deep breaths.

Let the war begin, she thought. 'Now we may entertain any questions.'

The hands erected instantaneously. She took her time to pick. Strategically better early than later, she picked Brenla. Brenla delayed for a while particularly surprised of being the first one to be selected.

'How many people have been destroyed because of Science, Yana?' Brenla let out.

'I wouldn't practically know the number, Brenla, I don't have the statistics and I doubt if genuine ones exist,' Yana replied carefully.

'But you assumed that many have died because of Religion and Culture, wasn't that so?' Brenla fought.

'I did and that is true.'

'And yet again you claim that you don't have the stats?' Brenla grinned at her.

'Yes, I claim that as well, that is true.'

'I don't get it here. Your info must be biased is it not, Yana? How can you know something about other things then compare them with the other which you don't know anything about?' Brenla went for the jugular vein.

Yana remained calm much to the other's surprise. Lotando knew Yana to be most difficult to thaw when calm. It would be nice to get her pissed first. 'Not biased, but logical, Brenla. You are defending the notion that my statement isn't true, biased as you say?'

'Definitely, Christianity fears no borders. It has saved more lives than any Science or Culture,' Brenla emphasized confidently.

'Then, Brenla, tell me, how many vaccines have Christianity invented to save the millions of people out there to supplement those killed in religious battles? I need the name of the Christian Society and those who created your named *vaccine* please, or, to be fair, even a pill of relief,' Yana put forward.

Checkmate, Chenai thought, *damn you, Yana.* She knew that was the best answer of the day. Brenla squirmed and amazingly didn't say anything anymore. Hands shot up.

'Er – I'll have one from Culture, Ash,' Yana said. She had to take care of familiars first, and then deal with the rest later.

Ash smiled. 'Can you please tell me how Science began, Yana?'

Yana smiled back. *You clever boy,* she thought, *but I'm not Brenla, I'm indeed a scientist, don't you know?*

'Science is excessively under-defined to relate its source of origin. Its source dates back to the Greek philosophers, the Egyptian mathematicians, the Renaissances kings – only to mention a few.'

'Didn't these people have a certain type of culture, an origin in which they followed and helped to preserve? You mentioned the Greeks, the Egyptians and more. They must have been different in some way, weren't they?'

'Yes, they indeed were, very much diversified in many spectrums,' Yana said softly. *What are you getting at?*

'And they call those different spectrums by a word in English, which is –? I'm sure you know,' Ash smiled some more. *Come on, Doc. Show me what you got.*

'They call it Culture, of course, didn't you know? I thought that was your topic,' Yana said, seemingly acting surprised, and laughter filled the air.

'I know my topic, Yana,' Ash laughed as well. Yana smiled back. His sense of humour was unique and she knew he was just getting warm. 'But do you know where yours came from. Where did Science come from?'

'Frankly speaking, all science comes from the combination of different cultures.'

Ash was stunned. 'You admit?'

'Yes, I admit very much. Science is there because many cultures fused to form a beautiful subject, Ashley,' Yana said in a confident tone.

Ash smiled. *Got you!* 'Now you must want to eat your words for you now see and admit that with no Culture, no people, there would be no Science. They are correlated in many ways, Science and Culture.'

Yana laughed and this unnerved Ash. Yana stopped abruptly and sighed. 'They may be correlated, but *without science there is no culture to be remembered.* Culture exists because it's preserved by the refrigeration of the definition Science. Culture doesn't offer painkillers created from various chemicals discovered by Science to sooth pain. People who formed science through their cultures hundreds of years ago are long decayed. Most of their cultures are long decaying. So how can something that is no longer capable of sustaining itself to survive existence be the basis of humanity? *Science is humanity,*' Yana told him and the others looking.

She was just incredible, and she hadn't even used her *bullets,* which were proudly smiling behind her. Hands went up, but they were less.

'I'll take another one from Christianity,' Yana picked. 'Diana.'

'Thank you, I've one small question to ask,' she said in a low voice. 'Let's say for assessment sake Science didn't exist, in a calm world with fair distribution, who would live better?'

Yana looked at her confused. She swiftly made a choice. 'I guess the Christians would live better.'

'And if these Christians live better, what would happen if you gave them a gun? Just one gun.'

Yana was no more confused. Diana was older. She must be surely smarter. 'If anything would go amiss, someone would use the gun to aggress.'

'And if, let's say,' Diana continued, 'we provided them with a nuke and one of them happens to accidentally accentuate it in hope of learning about its scientific nature. What would happen then?'

Yana knew defeat, but she replied. 'No Christian will be left in a hundred miles.'

'What created the nuke, what created the gun? Did Christianity create the nuke or was it Culture?' Diana asked in an even voice.

Yana swore inwardly. *Okay you win there.* 'It was Science.'

'Meaning more people would live if Science didn't exist despite the many it saves. Thank you, Yana, I got my answer.'

Everyone beamed excluding the ones on stage. Yana gave

an acknowledgement nod. The Christians were satisfied. Brenla beamed. *Doctor that Doc.* No hand came up from the Christians. They were celebrating revenge. However, one did come up from the Culture bench.

Yana slumped. *Not you,* she thought demented, *and I thought we were sisters.* 'Er – Lot.'

'Thank you, Yana,' Lotando said graciously. *You brought me here. I'm not going to forget that, Nana.* 'Science is humanity and humanity is science, you said?'

'Yes,' Yana rather whispered.

'Science is a better means of maintaining humanity than Christianity and Cultures, is that true?'

'Yes!' Yana replied more firmly. *Get on with it!*

'Thanks, that's all I needed to know,' Lotando said.

The air remained still for a while. *What is it with this girl? Why did she even ask? Maybe she didn't want to embarrass her cousin sister,* a lot thought. Yana thought differently. She cursed Lotando. Lotando knew that she hated guessing, but that was Lot – always left you guessing. Those questions had annoyed her more than anything else had. *Tomorrow will be your day. I hope they let you centre the stage sister.*

CHAPTER TWENTY

Roots Approval

During the three days, it was impossible to think about anything except the debates. Lotando thought it was much as ever an interesting an activity she had had in years. She suddenly began to think that Yana had been wise to have persuaded her to be part of this camping. She was more relieved nothing out of the ordinary had transpired and the twins were currently looking much better. She also had fun seeing the medic assistant expertly court her cousin. They looked lovely together. She could discern signs of attraction effusing between other members like Brenla and Never, Chenai and Winster – pre-assumed though – and Ash and Shamiso.

Due to the different groupings, only Brenla and Never seemed to experience a much more advanced feeling. That was currently all she could put a private finger on. Despite their purposes of being associative, the groups had become competitors. No one wanted to be seen talking to anybody from another group although this was possible during bath time or when sleeping time came. Lotando learned much more about their associates from Mutare than she had wanted to. Some of it was saddening, some intriguing.

That second week's Friday, the Culture camp made the stage. Daniel took the stand and smiled at them. He was forced to be the leader he was. After what had happened to Yana and Brenla, nobody wanted to be spokesperson for anything. They knew that their topic was the weakest to defend, rather explain. Twelve people sitting down there were eager to hear the words *questions please*. However, his group had designed a plan and Lotando was its *analyst*. It was much easier and less harm consuming. The priests and medic were quite entertained by the debates that they had jot their notepads with interesting notes about each essential. The occasion had first begun as a simple seminar. It was fiercely turning into a battle of supremacy.

'Good afternoon, brothers, sisters and Fathers. Don't we all have a father and mother, don't they all have their own fathers and mothers, and don't those fathers and mothers have their own parents? Where we come from is vital. Where did Jesus come from, where did the Greeks, scientists and all come from. Didn't they have a father and a mother as well? For us to be, we come from something and obviously without that something, we can't become. That's culture, that's humanity. Nobody just came to be from thin air. I thank you, any questions?'

This received soft applauses from the Reverends and even the amused medic. The twelve below didn't even remember to breath. Culture surely didn't waste time trying to explain itself. It just explained itself.

'Ah, no questions, lovely, thank you,' Daniel said swiftly.

The Culture group stepped off stage like quicksilver. The others actually noticed what had happened too late. *Confuse them first and leave them wondering.* It was as if they hadn't even heard the speech for their minds registered nothing. This meant that no questions, meant understanding and, in this case, surrendering to the idea. It made them very stupid.

At 18:03 P.M. that same day, they sat in their different corners eating rice and chicken. They were now used to these categories of meals, even the twins who had first campaigned for *sadza* to be included on the menu. However, this kind of dish was one of the perfectly selected ones. It saved a lot of trouble associated with cooking, dish cleaning and quantity placement. Rice only needed one big pot on the fire with water, a little bit of salt and that was it. The chicken and soup were much easier than vegetables. In fact, they had carried none fresh with them in case they would wilt. They were taking it well and their supplies were still holding enough to support them till the final week.

'Lot, you are amazing,' Daniel smiled and bit off a chicken rib. 'It actually worked.'

Lotando smiled at her empty plate. She had finished eating and seconds to her was a thing for the twins. 'I told you that it would work. It works every time.'

'Who taught you that?' Ash asked, curious.

'Uncle Urey.'

'Oh, your uncle,' Ash sighed. 'I should have known. Did you look at Brenla and her crew? They looked like they were seeing a ghost or something.' The others laughed.

'They were, but the funny thing is our Daniel looks more like any ghost to me,' Ian quipped. Laughter continued.

'But Yana's approach was more elementary,' Godfrey alleged. 'You are sisters and Mr Urey must have taught her a thing or two.'

'Nana rarely listens to her father. She claims he is a mental manipulator who never makes straightforward sense in what he says. I in turn tend to observe and learn,' Lotando informed.

They continued talking until it was about seven-thirty when they gathered around the fireplace. It was time to take a recap on the past two weeks with the priests. Many arguments sparked as each group member defended his or her group's topic.

The campers woke up on Saturday very eager to take the presumed exciting hike. Their groups were making up and breaking up. It was a *marriage of divorces*. Tension sparked just like they would in soccer, basketball or any other competitive scenario. It had turned into a battle of minds to some extent. Each individual had devoted themselves to their topic. Nobody wanted to finish off three wonderful weeks second to anyone, worse third to everyone. It was all about pride and all of them had pride to protect. The priests were intrigued by their commitment.

Lotando knew that it wasn't practically normal. She currently understood why lawyers did their job. It didn't matter if they were correct or wrong, the compensation *sang real* and they stuck to their side no matter how silly it was or seemed. This was a need not a want and it wasn't negotiable.

Late morning – at about fifteen minutes to eleven – the groups walked accordingly in the direction of the Nyangombe Waterfalls. They had heard about it long back from the priests and were enthusiastic about it. Eager to see it, they had all chosen that day to do so. The crews carried with them a few relief resources including bottles of energy drinks, water and a few snacks to munch along the way. The Nyangombe Waterfalls, named after the river, was about six kilometres from the Chamber. The aged Father Mango had declined the offer to go along, systematically leaving Father Rosina with no choice, but to stay behind to keep him company.

Derrick had come along just in case anything hapless was to occur. Evidently, he walked with the second group, about fifty meters behind the leading group. In an orderly fashion, the Christians led the way following Father Mango's theoretical directions and an old map. The Scientists followed and the Culturists occupied the rear.

Apparently, it seemed like the Christians led by Brenla were walking faster as they talked. The following day was the last day to prove the authenticity of their topic. They probably had no time to enjoy the climb to the waterfalls. They didn't mix topics with pleasure. The following day was a do or die situation. They had to show fiercely that their topic was more superior. Their leader was asking many questions and they responded in every way they could master.

'What can we truly say about Christianity that will keep their mouths glued like Culture did?' Brenla was very anxious. She took a full swing on her bottle of water number two. It was cool, but it seemed like they were in a desert to her. 'Does anyone have any new ideas, Diana? Last time you showed some stuff.'

Diana gloomily shook her head. She tugged her black jacket down to cover her long skirt's upper region. She despised the attention it was being given by Never, who just couldn't look anywhere else.

Deprived off the lower sight, Never curved his attention to the owner's face. Diana sulked. She *hated* men.

Brenla saw this and was infuriated. *Wasn't everything about her enough for the guy?* She had thought that at least something was alight between the two of them. *Was it blind attraction?*

'Never, any contributions, any new brilliant ideas?'

Never looked at her trying to conceal his embarrassment at being caught salvaging somebody's great everything. That was meant to be someone's attention and that someone lacking it wasn't so pleased of not receiving it.

'I'm trying to think, give me a moment,' he said.

Brenla frowned. 'I can see that you are trying. Keep it up, we might actually get somewhere.'

Never shrugged, but said nothing. He tried not to be caught again. *Damn, you are all so hot,* he thought admiring Brenla's all black attire for the first time.

'I think I got an idea, Bren.' It was Tawanda *part 2*, now *Kheda* to the others.

'What is it, Tawa?' Brenla asked merrily projecting her attention away from Never.

Kheda beamed. He was being tormented by that braided hairstyle Brenla wore, those soft nice brown eyes, that feminine nose and that perfect mouth that produced a Grammy Award winning voice. He had to admit, God didn't make them as much better than what he was seeing. He was swiftly getting possessed and it didn't get any better. Brenla's eyes were enchanted by Never. Never was however painfully having a hard time of choices. It showed that age and experience didn't matter in these things. *Love knows no talents. How could Brenla like Never, whilst Never had it big for Diana at the same time by which Diana didn't give a shit?*

Try all you want mate, he thought, *With D, it's a fairy tale that will never happen, bro. Believe me, I was wise enough not to try.*

Diana gazed at Kheda. She frowned. This was probably the fourth time she had caught him staring at their leader. She knew that part of her wasn't supposed to flare, but still she couldn't deny the fact. She wished those four times had been hers, and maybe, just maybe she would make him never look at anyone other than her like that no more.

Lotando couldn't believe herself laughing. She thought it was *biased.* That word was concentrated in her head as of late. The idea that it wasn't the twins making her laugh was amusing. Their leader was a real funny amusing character, once he warmed up to you. He wasn't so scared of her it had turned out.

His life was simple. He was indeed an orphan living with Father Mango's sister, his kind adopted mother and a successful accountant at his age. Although he didn't disclose anything about his biological parents, Lotando felt that he was one of those unfortunate kids born of a desperate mother and left to become the burden of someone else. Lot had never known she could feel life like this.

The twins were up ahead having a cultural debate with Ash. Ash was laughing all the way up. Godfrey had suddenly disappeared, budding ahead to the Science group. This was treachery, but Godfrey knew that time was of the essence. He had to make a move now otherwise he was sure he would regret it for the rest of his life. Emotions weren't something to mess around with.

Lotando laughed again, and she felt it again. She looked at him to see his eyes. No luck. He talked whilst staring forward or looking downwards. He was avoiding eye contact with her. *But why with me? We are alone here.*

I wish you didn't look so good, Daniel thought. *I can't even pronounce my words clearly. I would have loved to speak in Shona for now, oh, man.* He thought of trying to steal a glance at her face again, just once and maybe something to remember. A picture of her face in his mind was treasure at the moment and he didn't have a clear one. He tried and realized his mistake too late. She was looking directly at him. Their eyes locked. What they felt at that particular moment, only they could tell, no one else.

Only a year younger, Chenai thought, *a few months younger to be direct. However, he is still at school. It never means much, only blind silly feelings, we are still young.*

Chenai trod over a stone and got assistance from Kheda. She smiled thanks at him. Kheda was good looking, but the person on her mind was just perfect for her. By no means had anyone suppressed such emotion. She liked that. A dude who was true to his word and who by no means misunderstood a true feeling. She just wished she was back there listening to his crazy ideas. She always had lots of fun with Winster, as of recent. Her friends at her former school had always boasted about how it was so cool to exchange tongues with boys, to exchange their faces like underwear, to boast about how the first time experiencing the famous rubbing action when totally immature and irresponsible to gain that first experience was cool. She had once tried to follow, but her parents had limited her well. She had never exchanged tongues, never ever taken in a face to remember, and definitely never had sex. In her nineteen years, she had never had a boyfriend. Peterhouse Girls College had made sure of that. She wasn't proud of it, neither was she ashamed of it. Soon, she would turn twenty and it would be a record in the Muchemwas.

'Hi, my name is Godfrey.'

Shamiso smiled gazing back at him as he tried to keep pace with her. *Brenla's brother, what an intro.* 'After two weeks, didn't you somehow expect me to know it?'

Godfrey smiled shyly. *Just like the chicks at college, soft tone means soft response, very welcome and feeling the guy.* 'Thought with all the dudes around, you'd probably miss it.'

'How can I miss it?' Shamiso crooned. 'Godfrey, Godfrey, Godfrey,' she sang in a repeated chorus.

Godfrey breathed hard. It sounded so sweet from her lips. He felt a cold shiver penetrating his toes. 'So, Shamiso, tell me. What brought a beautiful woman like you to this dull place?'

'Dull place, you are here aren't you, Godfrey?'

Please stop that, Godfrey couldn't bear her saying his name like that. It was so seductive. 'I like dull, it's exciting,' Shamiso laughed some more. The other scientists looked back at them.

What are you doing here Godfrey? Yana thought furiously. *Trying to smuggle our ideas, hey?* She glared reproachfully at Shamiso. Shamiso glared back at her smiling reassuringly. Yana's fury faded. She knew she could trust her. But back somewhere someone wasn't at all pleased. Ash felt a huge note rise up his throat.

Crap, crap, he thought. *Damn you, Hewstone.*

'You like our youthful sister don't you, my man?' Ignatius said out of nowhere.

'Can't take your big eyes of her, Ash?' Ian added.

'Huh?' Ash was stunned.

'You like Shamz hey, Ash?' Ian was cheeky.

Ash grinned. He was just too weak and furious to deny. He had planned everything, the date being the previous day, and he had gotten more than he had prayed for. He hadn't however implemented the plan, but then someone had soiled up his luck.

It was as agonizing as this. He had been filling the twenty litre water containers at the spring. They were about ten of them. The other guys acting as musclemen had gone off to unload the other filled ones and he was left with the empty ones yet to be filled. It was all him and the silent spring. Then he had heard the crinkling of soft drink bottles coming from the direction of the Chamber.

He had looked up and saw her all cool in a white top, a blue skirt and pink flip-flops. Varied from the other girls who had braided their hairs, she had pulled hers back. She was carrying three empty coke bottles with her. His tongue seemed as if it had been glued to the top of his mouth. He had managed to gulp, and stare. Polite or not, he had enjoyed himself every second.

'Oh, sorry,' Shamiso had sort of giggled. 'Tawanda right or Ash

– Lotando calls you that a lot.'

His tongue had mercilessly released itself at the right moment. 'Well, Lot is lots of a lot if I must say something about her too.'

Shamiso had laughed. A nice laugh and it had matched everything about her. *God is surely missing a cherub up there,* he had thought. Shamiso had bent down to fill the bottles with water. One of them had suddenly slipped from her grasp and was about to be deposited into the spring. Ash had gone for it. Shamiso had also automatically reached for her falling bottle. Ash had only managed to grasp it before its downfall and Shamiso had only managed to slip off balance and was about to fall barely inches away into the spring.

Tawanda had caught her just in time and, in a kneeling posture, had pulled her back with all the strength he could master as she leaned over. He had held her back, like cuddling a baby.

Shamiso had looked into his eyes with passion and had amazingly giggled and smiled. Tawanda had smiled back. Their faces had only been centimetres apart and none of them had wanted to reduce or increase that gap. The sound of a clearing throat had suddenly come.

'Er – sorry, I hope I'm not interrupting anything,' Father Rosina had said.

Pondai and Colodia, as genuine friends since the age of seven, enjoyed their gossip analysing moments. They looked up and laughed, then down and giggled.

'I think we're just getting warm,' Pondai claimed ruffling his dreadlocks.

'I think warmer,' Colodia giggled, adjusting her spectacles. Pondai read her mind and giggled too.

'I wish we could debate on *love,*' Pondai whispered. 'Then all of us wouldn't have to differ.'

'You are really that jealous hey, Rasta?' Colodia chided heaving herself to his back, compelling him to carry her.

Rasta didn't refuse. Instead, he got hold of her thighs and carried her like a baby. 'Who, me?' he mimicked, struggling to climb up a steep mound with Colodia's weight gravitating him backwards.

Colodia put her hands around his neck in fear of losing balance and falling. 'I know you, our medic is surely doing a good job, you wish.'

Pondai looked ahead and saw Yana enjoying herself with Derrick. Both were medical scholars, both walking and understanding each other.

I'm a sales executive with a civil engineering degree working for my filthy rich father, absolutely no chance. He said nothing, but he knew Colodia read every sentence in his mind. Colodia was like a sister to him. About fifteen years with her made her his closest pal, closer than his stupid father, drunkard brother and bitch of a sister. Only she could tell exactly what he felt and thought at any time.

'Guessed as much,' Colodia sighed. 'What about carrying me up to the falls and I'll put in a good word or two about you at girls' gossip time.'

'You are on,' Pondai ran for a few meters up and then released himself from the burden. They both stooped, panting and laughed for a while before continuing.

Some of the Harare crew who didn't know the connection between the two surely had nothing in mind as they saw these two suddenly acting like this. They assumed they were two people who weren't too shy to show their true love openly. Less they didn't know that materially these two shared another kind of love. It was true, true love, but not their ideal kind of love.

CHAPTER TWENTY – ONE

Merit Enlightenment

Brenla and her team had led them in a complete circle. They had found no waterfall. The people who were supposed to have been listening when Father Mango had given the directions to the *Nyangombe Falls* had been annoyingly absent minded. They had walked a good eleven kilometres altogether for nothing.

After deciding to return, after no success on the first six or so kilometres, they had carefully followed the trail back to the Chamber, which had been astoundingly faster. The Chamber was the easiest to locate since it was situated on high altitude.

Then, the groups had merged into one, walking faster back home not wanting to let the sun sink on them in this unfamiliar territory. The notion that the region was close to a National Park was the main motivator and possibly the only.

Derrick glanced at Yana amused. *She looks even more stunning when she is so damn serious,* he thought. They were now familiar with each other. She knew some about his family and he knew all about her family. For these past few days, they had experienced a new kind of bonding. The chemistry was so agreeable. However, their lives had become to be what they were today following different paths. He had been raised in the high-density suburb of Mbare. Anybody who knew that you came from Mbare would envision a disorganized facility full of the less fortunate individuals. The latter was authentic on his part.

His father had been killed in a bar brawl. His mother had been a merchandiser. Fortunately, his mother had somehow managed to get him through primary education without difficulty. His father's welfare pension funds had been part of that aid. Trouble had emerged when he became an Ordinary Level candidate. The residential rents had skyrocketed and he was forever grateful that he had managed to write his Ordinary Level exams without attending class tuition. He had read his books for a kid who loved knowledge and its wisdom and he was rewarded. Getting straight As at his O-levels had managed to win him a scholarship for A-level and university from the church. He had succeeded admirably and had attained a doctor's license. So far, he was waiting for the passing of his visa and work permit to go to work for United Nations in conjunction with the church at an organization in Norway. He owed his life's success to the church. He was a truly devoted Christian.

But Yana, Yana was born rich. No sad stories to relate about, no tales of financial constraints. She had gone to the best schools the country had to offer and was soon going to be a doctor like him. It was funny how lives lived. It was all about faith and he was currently helping on this Youth Camp because of two things. He owed the church and had nothing to do yet whilst waiting for his visa. It was unbelievable that two whole weeks had passed so swiftly. They felt like they had come yesterday.

The Sunday's midday sunlight enhanced the Chamber's main arena. The others sat below as the ones on point sat above. It was time.

Lotando glared at the leader of the Christianity group preparing for her last stage act, her final chance to brew and conquer supremacy. Brenla looked composed, relaxed and ready.

'Ms Hewstone, you may begin,' Father Rosina said.

The priests had done a good job by doing nothing on that tour. *On the previous ones, it was the bread and grease of the priests to spend the duration teaching and replying numerous questions from the youths.* Now it was the opposite. The teachers were gleaning lessons from the youths.

'I hereby stand representing my group and topic as its essential leader,' Brenla began. 'Allow me to bring up some three major topics in life – Love, Humanity and Responsibility. *"For God so loved the world that He gave us His only begotten Son, that whoever believes in Him should not perish, but have everlasting life".* God is love. He relates to us out of His own heart of love. There is nothing we can do or will ever do which isn't motivated by a selfless, sacrificial love. Have we not all one Father? Did not one God create us? That God came to our world as a real person. The person is Jesus. Jesus is the image of the Invincible God. So if you believe in Jesus, you believe in God, you believe in Christianity, you believe in love, humanity, you have attained a responsibility. Jesus is God made visible. Rough fishermen dropped their nets to follow Christ and small children flocked to receive His blessings. Why can't we attain the responsibility left for us, that Jesus died not only to give us a happier life now, but also to give us eternal life? Yet, we still craft the word *bias* to his name – you of little faith.'

A couple of benches below, the two priests nodded in agreement. They were feeling Brenla's speech to the bone.

'We need not doubt the importance of Religion, especially Christianity. We doubt these, we also doubt the Bible. We contradict the prophets of God who wrote it. We hear not their prophetic messages. But then you may still ask can we trust the Bible, can it be trusted, and is it reliable? The accurate fulfilment of the Bible's predictions shows that we can trust the Bible. You must understand that prophecy of Scripture came about the prophets own interpretation. *For prophecy never had its own origin in the will of men, but men spoke from God as the Holy Spirit carried them along,* I quote from 2 Peter one-verse-twenty to twenty-one.

For those who assume that Christianity is biased, my brothers and sisters, you should at least look upon the history of His prophecy. Christ's life is a fulfilment of prophecy, His place of birth, His lineage from the tribe of Judah prophesized by Genesis, His rejection prophesized also by Isaiah and His betrayal and the fee paid to His traitor, His death on the cross – all prophesized by the book of Psalm. The evidence is strong that Jesus didn't just happen to fit a few predictions. His biography was indeed written beforehand by supernatural means. Truly Jesus is the Son of God,' Brenla smoothly closed her Bible. She stared at the listeners for a while.

'Without Christianity, there is no true love. Jesus taught us how to love each other, how to forgive one another, how to associate in peace. Where there is no love, there is surely true conflict, biased minds and ungrateful hearts. We look at *love*. We all know about love,' the crowd murmured some bit. Brenla smiled. 'Love is extraordinary and it's free. It doesn't need culture or science to be formed. It needs a peaceful heart, and it needs a human being. Money can never buy true spiritual love. It can buy the physical part, but never the former. Cultural compelled marriages oppose this fact. They create biased love, hatred in societies and an imbalance of emotion. Science is trying so hard to find a way of making up for its mistakes by thin rubbers to save lives. Why? Because they claim that loving causes a deadly aspect we call AIDS – a possible lab mistake or man-made creation gone viral. Science tries to offer numerous scapegoats from being faithful. Now tell me, is that true love? Is that responsibility? You can never be faithful without faith. We can't wash off our sins with soap like dirt.'

Brenla's face was now puffed with emotion. She was now speaking sincerely. Many knew that when she had closed the Bible, she had closed the group's discussions. It was now all up to her to tell them as it was as a true leader defending her topic.

'How can Science be the basis of humanity whilst it is a ticking bomb patiently waiting to destroy it? How can Science say it is creating a protective resource whilst it is encouraging more death by that very same resource? We build arms of war to defend ourselves, from whom? We defend ourselves from ourselves. Many say it's our Culture to fight for what is ours. We kill each other and do other numerous things unspeakable over reasonless beliefs. Christianity is pure white like a dove. I thank you.'

The others clapped. It was a well-strung speech. They eagerly waited for her call.

'I'll take any questions please?' Brenla said likewise. The hands didn't shy.

Father Rosina stood up from behind them. 'Please, these are the last of our debates. Due to the hearing process, Father Mango and I have thought that it would be wise not to repeat questions from before.'

More hands went up.

Brenla thought twice on her first pick. 'Yana,' she picked with an unbelievable calmness.

'Brenla, finding solutions to scientific problems isn't a sin. Science makes your so-called rubbers to preserve humanity,' Yana stated. 'If there was no Science, there would be no thin rubbers and that would increase the number of people infected with the virus, more people to feed in population increase. Isn't there a need for Science to participate? What has Christianity got to do with the manufacturing of rubbers?'

A couple of guffaws filled the air. Lotando looked on amused.

Godfrey the more stunned. His sister showed no signs of anxiety, unrest or anything. She was as calm as he had never witnessed her before.

'Let me state my point clearly to you, Yana. If people have uncontrolled sex nowadays, the result is nothing other than AIDS or as you stated, population increase. If people fear AIDS, what will they do? They will behave themselves leading to less AIDS donors. This is in other words called being *faithful and abstaining*, this is Christianity. Then if people search for an alternative and they develop things that can possibly save you from getting the virus whilst indulging in naughty practices, what will people do now? They will not behave. They will chance it because it's a speculative risk. Without the rubber, it would be a pure risk, and less people are that stupid enough to take them. The more Science creates rubbers which are never 100% guaranteed safe, the more people at risk. The more birth control pills created for the people, the more teenagers who take pregnancy risks, and then the less faithful we all become. You know something, dear sister – humans are very stubborn. You tell them rubber will save you, and what do they do? They claim you are rubbish. They try no rubber attesting their reliability and their luck. Understand now, Yana?'

Yana was completely stunned. *Did she just call me dear sister and really mean it? This is unbelievable. Bretty has suddenly grown a heart overnight.* 'I understand,' she rested her case.

'You're going to be a Doctor soon, I'd expect you to,' Brenla complemented. 'Questions please, er, Danny.'

Daniel beamed. Lotando was ignited. She felt a rush somewhere in her nose and beneath the thorax. Brenla's gaze at Daniel was exaggerated.

It was astounding really, to wake up on the other side of the camping bag. During tea, before the last Sunday service held by Father Mango, Daniel and Brenla had amazingly talked for too long, Lotando assumed.

'I'd like to know something, Bren,' Daniel, back to the present, asked. 'Why do we love those we love?'

Yana smiled. Ash silently applauded. *Too much time spent talking to Lotando,* he thought. Lot had a tendency of replicating and double emending questions. It was like, *are you Tawanda who is that Tawanda?* It took time to decipher it all, but in the end, he had to admit, it was roughly philosophically innovated.

Brenla however answered without resting in faith. 'We love those we tend to love because they are the ones we choose to love not who we are supposed to love. This is wrong in Christianity as it clearly defines loving thy enemies. Science tends to love its friends whilst it hates its enemies by creating their downfalls. On the other hand, Culture is optional on choice. Universal appeal doesn't get a review as far as it is concerned.'

Brenla looked reborn, like a new St. Brenla. She spoke with that full throttle confidence capacity. Two hands were up this time. 'Shamie.'

'Thank you. Is there any difference in being a Christian and being a politician? There are things such as the Jihad, Holy Wars. Holy does mean religious?' Shamiso asked. The others nodded in agreement.

Brenla systematically said. 'I'll let Tawanda answer that one for you, Shamie,' she said, giving Kheda the stand.

'A Christian is a follower of the Christianity doctrine. A politician is a social activist. Politics differ, Christians differ, but politics differ overall whilst Christians agree on one thing that is of major importance. This is to follow the ways of Jesus Christ our Lord. Do I satisfy your inquiry ma'am?' Tawanda asked flirtatiously, eyes straight at her sizing her up.

Good Strategy, Pondai thought. *Thaw the lady to shut up whilst she is still warm.*

'Thank you, I do understand,' Shamiso answered sounding gratified.

Only one hand shot up.

'Lot,' Brenla picked her. 'Fire away.'

Lotando tried to smile back at her. Brenla and her team had finished off well. They had prepared fully and probably deserved such a splendid conclusion.

'Thank you, Brenla. If I may, how can we be certain that the Bible wasn't rigged?'

This derived some murmurs. *How best can a question be so controversial and come from the mouth of a lady?*

As if planned, Tawanda returned to sit whilst Diana came forward to mount the stand. Her eyes had an interesting sparkle about them. She opened Brenla's Bible to a certain reading. She took a few seconds and then closed it back. Diana looked back at the listeners below.

'There are many theories that claim that the Bible isn't whole,' Diana started to explain, 'but these theories are as empty as their claims. The Bible is actually a library of sixty-six books. The prophet Moses wrote the first five books of the Bible, businessmen, shepherds, fisherman, soldiers, physicians, preachers, philosophers, human beings from all occupations contributed to the Great Book. They all lived with contrasting cultures and philosophies. But then, some of these had never met each other, but it seems like they were all made up of one mind – the mind of God. The question of it being rigged must surely be a joke.'

Silence followed. Lotando thought for a while then said. 'It is said by many that there are some respectable books which didn't qualify, or survive to be amongst the sixty-six books, yet they were written by well-established sages of the Great history which the Bible praises, especially some of them supposedly frowned their rightful place in the New Testament. Why then do you defend that something wasn't rigged whilst it was carefully carved to produce what those who edited and produced the Big Book found appealing, what suited them not all?'

For the first time, Diana looked into Lot's eyes, smiled at her and boy didn't she look stunning. What pleased Diana about the question was the fact that Lot had produced it from the heart. Diana admired those who spoke from the inner soul. She knew the young lady to be enthusiastic, and sometimes thought her to be the *wisest* of them all.

'Lotando, in this world we are living, all of us are contentious. It's something humans can't help being. People are forbidden to kill, are forbidden to steal, are forbidden from staining young minds with pornographic material, are forbidden to encourage bad habits, but then don't all of us come across all these things out in the open on a daily basis? For those who claim that there are many desirable books that must be included in the Bible to enlighten us into seeing some things they think we don't see, if they were so eager for the world to know it all, why haven't even one of those books been published? Why hasn't it been publicized to the people like music or art is done? Why not just leak the material on the internet and say, "these are the true writings the Bible has never shown?" Only one simple answer exists. There are no such writings. They are purely imaginative and disastrous thoughts.'

This received acknowledgment murmurs from the priests. Not

expected to take sides as they were, but they were Christians and nothing was going to change that.

Lotando thanked Diana for her answers. She didn't try her luck. She knew that Dee was older, mature and much wiser than any girl around. Although Diana always looked dull, not that kind of chatty type, Lot knew that behind all that beauty and missing light was a true spirit of intelligence. To know, you only had to look at the eyes, and so far, to Lotando, they had never lied. However, Lot could also see that hidden scars bothered those eyes. Only five more days and if she didn't find out then, Lot knew she would never know.

At dinnertime, it was time for the remaining groups to worry. Brenla had led her team to a great finish. It had made no mistakes, Christianity now ruled supreme. They didn't even need the full moon shinning in the sky to tell them that.

CHAPTER TWENTY – TWO

Creation Integration

After a series of threatening showers, the campers set up the tents. Overall, they comprised of eleven green tents that had come with the Mutare group, each with the maximum capacity intake of three people. At about a thousand meters above sea level, rain became an apparent anomaly during the final week. The mid days of April in these parts of the country were structured by frequent thunderstorms withering the grasslands and forest.

The fact that the fort had been built with no ceiling was actually confounding. They tried to discover why and how the people who had built the place had adapted, managing to survive the winters and rainy summer periods. Maybe in winter, the firewood helped as the masonry would absorb and radiate heat through the night, but what about in summer when the rains poured like hell? As far as they could see, there was practically no way one could sleep or shelter in such an environment in rainy seasons, but then there were numerous caves nearby. It could have been possible, but complex.

'Father, how did you become a priest?'

Father Rosina turned at his side of the tent. He looked at the tent's ceiling hearing the drizzle composing a faint rhythm on its exterior surface. It was probably around eight in the evening. He was sure that Father Mango was by now peacefully sleeping in his sole tent. He was an aged clergyman who needed his peace. Father Rosina wondered how Father Mango had become a priest. The elderly priest was now mature in the profession, the age that would be required for one to be a Bishop. Father Rosina doubted very much that the man would ever taste the high rank for *definite* reasons, but he projected the man to have made a great leader. It was too bad that Father Mango wasn't going to get that chance.

Father Rosina woke from his slumber to note that his silence might be mistaken for ignoring. 'The Lord works in mysterious ways, Derrick. God chose me to do his work in not such a pleasant way.'

Derrick read the notes in his voice to be mixed with undefined emotion. He knew less about the man. Rumours had it that, although he became a priest, there was a sad story behind it. He was very curious. This was maybe the only time to find out the real story from the man himself. He waited patiently wishing Father Rosina wouldn't stop there.

Fortunately, Father Rosina confided. 'My father was a Reverend in Johannesburg down South. My mother was an Evangelist in Namibia. They met at a conference one year in Johannesburg and married. Then they were all transferred to a new Anglican Church that was being built here in Zimbabwe. After my older brother was born, they moved to live here permanently. My young sister and I were born Zimbabweans and we learned the local language pretty well as we grew up. About twenty years later, I was attending a party with my former high school mates. The next thing I remember was arriving back home that night and was just in time to watch the last bits of our house collapse into ashes. The fire department had arrived too late and a huge crowd watched as the fire fighters tried desperately to lessen the damage. The fire carried with it my whole family. Every one of them was in the house as the investigation results proved. The cause of the fire was deduced to be an undetected short circuit in the kitchen. Three years later, after realizing that God had made me live for a reason I enrolled at the Theological College.'

Yana couldn't sleep. She didn't know why. *Was it because of her topic to be presented the following day or that something else?* She was confused, yet she knew she had to keep it cool or everything in her head was going to get ugly.

'You can't sleep, can you, Nana?'

Yana was startled. She had thought that Lot was asleep by now. The conditions were too nice to resist dozing off instantly. 'I can't, Lot, why are you still awake?'

Lotando shrugged. They were sleeping as a pair in a reserved spectrum like the others. 'I can't sleep either, I don't know why.'

'You know,' Yana couldn't believe it, 'that's exactly the way I am feeling.'

'Thinking about D?'

'Diana?'

'Not that D – you know the D I'm talking about. You two would make a perfect couple,' Lotando said shifting into a comfortable position in her sleeping bag.

'You think too much, Lot,' Yana produced a weak laugh. *My thoughts are much close than you can ever imagine,* she thought. She had to ask, perhaps now. Things had turned out very much different. 'Lot?'

Lotando knew her too well to decode her voice. Something was definitely up. 'What is bothering you, Nana?' she answered sympathetically.

Yana took a deep breath. 'You know, these days I have been thinking of Grandpa,' she progressed.

Lotando excessively felt something she hadn't felt in a long time. It made her shiver. 'What about him?' her voice was barely audible.

'I don't really know how to say it, but I think his untimely death is haunting me,' Yana said. 'I'm really trying, but it's too hard to believe that he is dead. I never knew that I loved him so much to feel this way.'

Lotando remained silent. She was struggling with an undesirable feeling. *What was this doing to her?*

'He must have had that stroke about something, the doctors said so,' Yana continued in a sadder tone. 'But what about, why did he stroke?'

Lot this time didn't answer. She tried to breathe as slow as unnoticeable as she could. *What are you about to ask me?*

'You were the last one who talked to him before he died, what did the two of you talk about?'

'People are naturally more interested in things and pictures than in abstract words. Even adults look through books for pictures. Visual aids have a greater impact than words alone. I'd like to say the Bible alone stands unfulfilled. I mean, without the pictures, the ideologies, the research and all that help to elucidate the Bible's meanings, it would barely be recognizable or understandable,' Yana spoke to the crowd below. She was eager to get this over. Her mind wasn't functioning well at the moment.

'Without Science, the Bible can't be reproduced and be distributed to the millions out there, thus the Word of God will be limited in spectrum. Without Science, the ink, the pictures, the movies that resemble holiness and spiritual growth wouldn't exist. So why are you Christians so damn selective when it comes to Science being the supreme resource base for humanity? Without Science, Christianity and Culture wouldn't even exist. Those books in the Old and New Testament were written because some scientists invented something called *paper, pen and ink*. We know and try to follow Christ's way because we have somewhere to refer to and that somewhere exists because Science existed.

Love? We are all humans and the fact that we are human means that we can't deny how we were created. To express love regards many processes, but the one involving the use of rubbers or unsheathed is as essential as faithfulness is meaningless. Not all people can be faithful. We were created differently, minds diversified. You can't separate an emotion from an individual, and you can't control someone else's emotion. Is it a sin to find a solution to stop the unfaithful from transmitting the deadly disease to the faithful? Husband unfaithful, wife faithful, in the end all are going to suffer. Therefore, Science puts an intermediary to try, at least, to save the good from suffering an undesirable fate caused by the unfaithful. Isn't that you Christians being saved by Science?

If AIDS is going to be cured, the cure will not come from Culture e.g. Norms and Beliefs or Attitudes, it is going to become because Science is. God created people, people created the disease and God will not at once just say a thing called AIDS no longer exists and that will be it. No, Science can find that cure. Only Science can assist those who want to be helped. Please, just at least look at how our topic has helped save humanity, love or responsibility. Compare the statistics. Assume the detrimental effects resulting in the absence of the other. People can't all be clerics, traditional leaders and royalty. Science creates jobs, encourages humanity. Genuinely speaking, Science-Religion-Culture correlate vitally, but all can't continue to exist without Science, but Science can continue to live without them – especially Culture. I thank you.'

The last statement infuriated the group sitting on the front row bench. Their hands twitched, waiting for Yana to ask for them. Amusingly, Yana exchanged positions with Winster whilst she went to sit on the stage's bench to watch. *Tag-team Urey.* The others below didn't wait for Winster to ask, their hands greeted him to the stand. All six hands from the Culture group were airborne. Winster shrugged. *Thank you sister for teasing them bees for me,* he shrugged. He took a long time to choose.

'Ian' At least they were of the same age.

'Thank you, Mr Winner,' Ian said. 'How can things correlate and then live without the other? How can a wife and husband agree in love and companionship whilst one of them doesn't even exist?'

Winster cringed inwards. *Now I'm really thanking you, Yana,* he thought. *What was the reason of twisting your words?* He thought of every suitable answer. 'Christianity and Culture, in this case, both exist, but a husband can live without a wife after she no longer exist, when she is dead and still love her spiritually.'

Marvellous, Chenai thought. *What a marvellous answer.* Lotando thought as much. She was positive that she wouldn't have answered such a question in such a way. Ian remained silent, his question had confused him the composer and the answer as well had done the same to him. He knew his mind wasn't fully functional. Something was definitely wrong with him. Hands shot up minus two from the Culture bench.

'Daniel,' Winster picked. He seemed harmless.

'Thank you – how many Christians were scientists and how many are and aren't?'

Winster pretended to be unnerved by the question. 'Many scientists weren't Christians. Scientists like Newton, da Vinci, and Galileo weren't Christians as history states and yet they are as famous as Christianity itself. Nobody can answer how many are or how many scientists aren't Christians today. It's practically impossible, yet I still claim that the Fathers of Science weren't Christians – at least the majority of them.'

'So if they weren't Christians they must have been something else?'

'Yes, they had their own cultures in themselves,' Winster confessed.

Yana groaned behind. *How can one be as stupid as to voluntarily enter into the lion's den naked?*

Daniel smiled and felt his excitement rising. 'So for there to be Science there has to be Culture?'

'Yes, I think that point has been clarified already.'

The others behind him couldn't bear to hear more. They were trapped.

'But your leader said earlier that Science can be without Culture, it can exist without there being Culture.'

Winster smiled and nodded. 'Culture is a broad term, Culture can't exist without Science the way money can't exist without the existence of man, but man can exist without the existence of money.'

Daniel was caught unawares, still celebrating victory too early to understand what Winster had said. He was silent for a while.

'Anymore questions, please?' Winster didn't give him the time to recover. 'Never.'

'Thanks – now why is it that Science and Christianity always differ?' Never asked. This was by large an ideal question.

'We aren't here to frown off Christianity. We believe Christianity is a vital Science of its own just as many Cultures are currently becoming obsolete in the meaning of the modern era. What we only claim is that Science is the major fuel behind humanity since Christianity can't individually be able to do so like it can.'

Six people couldn't believe the young man's nerve. Six others couldn't have been more pleased. It was like a merge, integration of differing transactions. Lotando was brilliantly stunned. Science had clearly descripted its approach upon Culture. It was like they courted and charmed Religion into giving up whilst on the other hand making sure that Culture was dead before it even started.

It was unnaturally coincidental that Yana, Winster and Jack were in the same group. From the Harare crew, it would have been undeniably fit to designate them as the cream smart heads. If it was a prize-winning contest, Lotando was sure that Religion had been coaxed off the top and Culture was thwarted. There was no way they were going to survive Science's pre-attack and there was no way Religion was going to redeem itself. *Damn these scientists,* Daniel thought. *We are so gone.*

'If there should be no more questions,' Winster said with a gratified sigh, 'we conclude by saying, *"let no Science be the distaste of humanity, but its glorious legacy."'*

CHAPTER TWENTY – THREE

Freedom of Truth

Lotando was trying hard to interpret why Yana was suddenly so uptight. If it had been her attitude towards only her, she would have understood, but it was apparent that Derrick was suffering the same fate.

Why had Yana suddenly dragged out such a nasty subject after so long?

Lotando knew grandfather and granddaughter had been tight. She had always been jealous of them. It was too easy to see that Yana hadn't recovered from losing Christopher Urey. Yana's love for her granddad had been far more than that she had reserved for her own father. Lotando knew that Yana would never understand, because she too was still trying to figure *it* out. Somehow, Lot felt that, after two enjoyable good weeks at the Torturer Chamber, something was wrong in the air. Their camping had an eerie concluding effect radiating from it. The day after tomorrow, they were all going back home.

Never was agitated. He had tried almost everything, but Diana was just too stony. It was clear that she didn't give a shit about him. All the three weeks were going down the drain. He wasn't used to this, but then this was different. For the first time, the feelings were genuine – or maybe it was the idea of her not being interested in him that made her very interesting to him. The lady was dull, but she had a great body, a perfect face and she looked his age. Theory used to say that those ladies your age weren't yours. They were for the old *madharas*. Yours were those two or more years younger than you were.

Fuck theory. He wished to prove it wrong, but he was very wrong. In fact, he thought they were all wrong. His *desire* had no eyes for him. She desired someone else. Annoyingly, that someone else had eyes for Brenla who had her eyes for him no more. It was warped. He began to envy Diana so much that he was on the verge of snapping. Never wished he had kept his eyes on Brenla until the end, because Brenla had lost her patience along the way and her eyes were now searching on Kheda.

Brenla knew Kheda had the hots for her, but then Diana had the hots for him. Brenla wished he would somehow find out soon before it was too late. She and Diana never talked much and she figured much of the hostility to have derived from this.

Lotando had never had a boyfriend before in the much deeper sense of a lover. Yana was amazed by the girl's clean record. She herself had been involved in numerous relationships. Hers had begun like fun and ended like fun. None of her ex-boyfriends had come out envious, seethed or disappointed. It had been worth a ride, and they had all happily moved on still managing to keep on being good friends with her. This was basically the fruits of choosing her guys with care. Yana knew that, that was the part of life Lotando had never opened up to enjoy. *Maybe things were going to change.*

Daniel mounted the stand. It was Thursday at two P.M. The cool breeze conditioned the Torture Chamber's atmosphere compelling its guests to dress warm. The twins, sitting close together on the stage's bench, shook like battery powered play dolls. Lotando, who sat beside Ian, couldn't help whispering to him to hush the act. Ian made the scene look more comical by muttering, *'I'm cold, Lot – are you cold, Lot? I'm cold a lot, are you cold a lot?"* continuously like a robot. Lot cursed under her breath. *I'm cold, but at least I'm human,* she thought

'Culture is where we come from. Science comes from Culture. Christianity comes from Culture. Our norms, values, our traditions, our lives are based on Culture. Love is a Culture. Attaining responsibility comes from having a culture to attain that responsibility. All humanity is Culture. It's astounding to realize that all of you don't see that or acknowledge,' Daniel first presented and passed the torch to someone else.

For the first time, a non-leader from the Culture group took the stand. They had done everything to make her. Lotando hated debates, hated conferences. In context, she despised anything that made her stand in front of a crowd to explain herself. No matter how small or familiar the crowd could be, it didn't appeal to her conscience.

She glared at the two groups sitting below, then at the priests and Derrick behind them. She felt herself shivering – she hated this. *Why had she agreed to do such a thing?* Daniel could have easily done this individually, but after Tuesday, nobody in her group had felt like talking about their grand finale. Instead, all had voted Daniel to present and Lotando to take over in a new fashion.

She felt very uncomfortable doing this, but her uncle had taught her a great *rule*. The best way to deal with it when you feel out of position was exactly to say what you thought about your situation. That approach could have gotten her expelled last month, but it had worked wonders. *Well, no one is expelled here,* she thought.

Brenla had been formidable. Yana had been formidable. Lotando knew she too had to give something memorable. She felt the eyes of her group perking her back, all waiting for her to take over. She shrugged.

'To tell the truth, I hate standing up here in front of you all to be defending a topic I definitely don't know anything or give a hell about,' she started.

Yana winced. Winster gaped. When Lotando spoke like the *genuine Lotando Urey,* she didn't give a damn about what the others would think about her. She spoke her mind out – all of it – and it always resulted in total unrest. This was that kind of Lot who was now standing in front of them. They looked down holding their breaths with the anticipation.

Lotando was on fire. 'And I'm glad I'm proud enough to admit it. It seems like all of you have the inconsiderate pride to be backing something you didn't really like to defend except perhaps the Christians – some of them I mean. Brenla and crew have the guts to claim that Science and Culture are anti-humanity. Yana and crew talks a lot, about how Science is the basis of humanity whilst frowning upon Christianity and Culture as nonsense. My crew and I are desperately trying to defend our topic without even knowing what we are really defending. I'd love to know why all of us spent all these days debating about things we don't know the real truth about.'

The last statement got to Brenla's nerves. She interjected instantly. 'What in the world is wrong with you? Your cousin sister is about to become a licensed Doctor in a few months. She knows

Science right through and she is defending Science. I know many things about Christianity, with the rest of my crew because, of course, we are all Christians. Just because you don't know anything about anything doesn't mean that all of us are that daft,' Brenla said heatedly.

'Oh, go to hell, Brenla,' Lotando retorted.

The pastors winced. *Now how did this turn into a bad ending?* Derrick couldn't help admiring Lotando's not give a damn attitude.

'Yana may be to become a doctor soon, but she isn't that much of what you would call a real scientist. I'm in that field – I know what a scientist is. And talking about you? Please don't make me laugh. You are just as much a Christian as I am not. It's amazing to look at all of you and then you say we know something about Science, about Christianity. We never look at the *reality* basis of this – the actuality of it, not the presumed. Reality is humanity – not Christianity, not Science or Culture. She says Christianity is the basis of humanity. What the hell is Christianity? I call it a term people hide behind, a term misappropriated and pronounced by people who fear to look at life in *reality* terms, hiding behind the cloak of Jesus Christ whilst they sin every second. Let's talk about the churches for a while,' Lotando's expression was that of anonymity. She couldn't stop herself from the sudden possession.

'How many churches are truly genuine today? None – it's all about political and monetary terms, hardly spiritual. People still abuse the church as a market place, maybe not for selling tomatoes, but for advertising image, selling fame and competing in investments. Churches have become moneymaking organizations for executives, gossip congregations for women, husband-searching facilities for desperate ladies looking for the right guy and the hunting ground for young men looking for innocent young church ladies. Worse, they have become psychological samples for politicians and hypocrites. Some have become conflict seeds, discrimination palaces. People are different, that's true, but you do say there is only one God and only one Jesus. So if there is only one God and one Jesus, one Bible, same Matthew, same Ruth and the same Isaiah, why the heck are there more than ten Christian churches, more than a dozen prophets, prophetesses – whatever they call themselves? Where is the unity there? Didn't Jesus encourage unity? Aren't we all people created of one image? Some say Science is the mother of humanity. Really, people? How can

Science be the mother of humanity since its people who created Science? No dog or lion ever invented anything. Without humans, Science wouldn't exist. Science is the daughter of humanity. How can one thing become the mother of one thing and become its child at the same time? Humanity, people, humans are the base of humanity. Not Christianity, not Culture, not Science.

Damn Culture, damn Science, and damn Christianity. Let's talk about more ideal stuff. Let's talk about the *totality of actuality*. Reality is what we see and try not to see. Has anyone here ever sat down and given some full thought about us, humans? How we live, how we associate, how we go about in our daily lives? Love! *Pure love is corresponding. For it to be, it needs two or more to be, never one.* I can't hate and love at the same time for neither will do me good. Experience maybe the best teacher in things like war where to live you have to be an expert in killing someone. In terms of love, experience is maybe the worst teacher, because the more heartbroken you become, the less love you expose. In my terms, love and experience don't cohere, so it doesn't cohere with Science or Christianity. It is better to be in love for the first time and that love is true than find true love after six douche bags. We can't talk about love being Science or Christianity without first talking about Unity. *No unity, no love.*

We are here being provided all this by the church, sponsors – enjoying ourselves whilst there is a child out there with an enormous bulging tumour needing immediate surgery, and who could use the funds we used to make this camp possible. There is a child out there being raped by his or her father, brother or relative in the process post getting pregnant or getting HIV. Another person of the same age, a Nicki Minaj wanna-be is somewhere living in plush Borrowdale having her hair done at an expensive salon later to join mummy and daddy at a tea party with the neighbours. An ignorant rich spoiled kid who cares nothing about his or her future spends a week's pocket money equivalent to someone's salary buying drugs and other shit. His or her parents send him or her to an expensive school for four years and that person manages to come out with disgusting grades. Guess what? The money the guy paid for one year of learning is more than adequate for someone less fortunate to spend all six years of education at a particular cheaper school. What does that person become? They work as an executive for one of daddy's or mommy's companies, sent to a university in Spain with nothing, but wealth's influence. Why does someone learning at a low-level school get failed intentionally or by mistake by an examination board after studying hard for a better life whilst at the same time, at a five times more expensive school, someone puts no effort and gets to become a doctor?

Has anybody ever walked in my hood? Eight would know. Or, do they hardly notice it – just how cool it is from the rest? Then has anyone ever passed through the high-density suburbs of Mbare? What kind of a world are we living in? Sometimes, I wonder, is God really that fair? Does he really exist? It's like those who do good die daily whilst those practicing evil almost live forever. What is the idea of taking away those people who help alleviate other people's suffering and leave those who increase the pain? Why do the rich get richer and the poor, poorer? The rich believe in God, the poor say he doesn't exist. Some rich don't believe in Him, a few poor depend and still look up to him. So, who is fooling who, you or me? Take it from a realistic point of view, *the good and happy die untimely and the bad and sad live forever.*

Why does a stray bullet kill a boy in the inner city of a gang street as he does his homework at the family's table? Why does a young mother in the suburbs find out that her child has contracted AIDS from a contaminated blood transfusion? Why does a faithful virgin of twenty-five get raped by a group of shitheads and directly gets the disease a week from getting married whilst a professional businessman who is a sugar daddy or a professional prostitute who has been in the game for more than ten years has got no AIDS on them?? Why do some girls look as cool as Brenla whilst some look like Tyson? Why does one girl in a poor family have less than a thirty percent chance of being beautiful whilst those rich children have more than a ninety percent chance of being gorgeous? Why are most good girls unfortunate to be raped whilst the opposite ones enjoy their lives and indulge into irresponsible immature sex? Why are some born crippled whilst some complete? Where is the bloody equality in that?

Why are the poor breeding more children, which they can't support, whilst the rich have few children? Is God really fair? The tragedies go on and on in the world. Where is God in a World of meaningless suffering and death? Psalm thirty-three verse five assures us that *"the earth is full of his unfailing love."* But, if that is true, why doesn't He bring an end to all this suffering and tragedy?

Priests, Derrick and all you brothers and sisters, if you answer these questions you'll see it my way. Call me an atheist, ignorant or whatever you may like, but the way I see it, we wasted three weeks discussing irrelevant issues instead of asking and answering these real questions. Despite my brothers and sisters from Mutare whom I'm glad I met and the resume reference credit I'm going to get for participation, I'm pretty pissed that I ever agreed to come here.'

CHAPTER TWENTY – FOUR

A Worldwide Message

They felt sad. The day was tomorrow. It surely was tomorrow. Mr Legondo was expected to come as early as ten in the morning to pick all of them up with three other drivers with Jeeps. On the day of arrival at the Chamber, Father Mango and his crew had arranged that they were going have to borrow some transport into the city of Mutare. All had been arranged since the Harare's crew bus was too big. The bonds that had been created, the new feelings that had been aroused and the information that had been gleaned, it seemed to have been worth it though the last speech had recently rocked their feet. The speaker too was feeling a little bumped. Her words had touched many hearts.

The Friday's air smoothened the oxygen as the star filled November sky progressed slowly towards eight o'clock. They were all sitting at the fireplace. As the debates were over, they sat independently, although a bench was reserved for the priests and the medic. They were all having a cup of tea or rather coffee for some. Lotando sat with Winster, Chenai, Ash, Shamiso and Ishmael.

Yana shared a bench with Pondai, Brenla, Daniel, Ian and Diana. Jack sat with Godfrey, Ignatius, Tawanda, Colodia and his brother. Since yesterday, after the controversial speech, conversations had extraordinarily become scarce. Momentarily, no conversations took place as they stared at the gleaming fire absent-minded.

'I guess you are all aware of our departure tomorrow,' Father Rosina broke the jinx. 'These past few weeks, I dearly hope were fun to you all. We learned and gave out a lot and I hope by knowing each other, we will keep the bond strong as we go. Many might be wondering which group came out on top. From what we saw and analysed, Father Mango, Dr Derrick and I thought it wise not to ruin the competition and call it a tie for all. As a man of the Almighty, I've some last precious words I'd like to share with you about Religion. My intent will be based upon the end of *False Religion*.'

Lotando shrugged holding her cup with both palms. She wondered if this was meant for her of little faith.

'There is a time when we have to ask ourselves some very important questions,' Father Rosina continued. 'Are we distressed about crimes committed in the name of Religion? Do warfare, terrorism, and corruption perpetrated by those who claim to serve God offend our sense of justice? Why does Religion seem to be at the root of so many problems?

The fault lies not with all Religion, but with False Religion. False Religion meddles in war and politics. Across Asia and beyond, power hungry leaders are cynically manipulating peoples' religions for their needs. False Religion spreads false doctrine. Most religions teach that the soul or spirit is some invincible part of a human that survives the death of the physical body. By means of this teaching, many of these religions exploit their members to pray for departed souls. False Religion tolerates immoral sex. *Don't be misled. Neither fornicators nor idolaters nor adulterers, nor even men kept for unnatural purposes nor will men who lie with men inherit God's kingdom.* In western lands, church groups ordain gay and lesbian members of the clergy and urge governments to recognize same sex marriages. Even churches that condemn children, have immorally tolerated religious leaders who have sexually abused children.

What does the future hold for Religions that produce rotten fruit? Like Jesus warned, *"Every tree not producing fine fruit gets cut down and thrown into the fire"*, it will be chopped down and destroyed. I encourage you all not to share the fate of False Religion and you can only have this within *True Religion*. How do you identify True Religion? True Religion practices love. Rather than killing one another, we should be willing to die for one another. This Religion trusts God's Word. Instead of teaching traditions and commands of men as doctrines, True Religion bases its doctrine on God's Word. True Religion strengthens families and upholds high moral standards. It trains husbands to love their wives, wives to develop deep respect for their husbands and teaches children to be obedient to their parents,' Father Rosina concluded his speech.

The youths gathered around looked onto him and felt as if they were truly non-believers, those of long lost faith – the sheep in disarray. It wasn't about Science, Christianity or Culture. It was about being human.

CHAPTER TWENTY – FIVE
Initial Sin

Ishmael, Never, Ash and Winster were just returning from having their final bath at their bathing sector. In line, Jack, Pondai, Daniel and Godfrey had dashed there to have quick baths before the last group. Becoming the first to enter the male's compartment, Never dried his hair with his long towel. He couldn't believe what he saw. He laughed.

'Hey, guys, come, quick,' he gestured to the other three. He pointed at three sleeping bags still occupied. 'These early birds are still cuddling. They don't want to leave their pants around.'

The others laughed fully entering into the quarters.

Ash threw his towel at Ian. 'Hey, wakey, wakey, old grit.'

Ian was dead asleep. He didn't budge an inch. *So much unlike him to let a tease unchallenged*, Ash thought nothing of it. He went straight for his bags and extracted a lotion bottle.

'Hey, give me some!' Winster begged, throwing his petroleum jelly bottle away. 'That smells good. No wonder you smell like a girl every time, bro.'

Ishmael and Never went over in anticipation. The four shared the bottle, changing their clothes in the luggage corner. The lotion had a remarkable nice scent, was pink in colour and smoothened slick on their different skins.

'Hey – don't drain it all up!' Ash cried as Never mercilessly squeezed the bottle.

'Take a niche, man,' Ishmael chuckled. 'We're leaving this place today. You must have plenty of this stuff back home.' Ash shrugged.

'Where did you buy this?' Winster suddenly asked. 'I thought this stuff was made for chicks.'

'That wasn't mine, it was my sister's,' Ash uncomfortably confessed. 'I borrowed it from her collection.' The others laughed.

'It smoothens so seductively when she puts it on –' Never said subconsciously, and then he forced his mouth shut. *Too late*

Ash eyed him curiously. *What the hell are you talking about?* 'How would you know that?' he glared at him.

The others could only guess how, they squirmed.

Never was older and shortly felt fearless. 'She has got a nice body growing on her whilst you get to see the whole of it live. The other girls make such a fuss about her Brazilian-like ass, you know. I wouldn't mind hitting that.'

Ash's jaw tightened – his insides molten with fury. He clinched his fists ready to pounce. There was only one way Never could have seen that. It would be so cheeky. Just sneak around an adjacent dark nook giving a clear view of the other wing's bathing sector and watch the ladies bath. It was so revolting to think about, but he knew Never might have probably done it more than twice since their stay at the Chamber. He knew Winster felt the same, but had the brains to leave it alone. He wondered what Godfrey could have done hearing the thought of someone peeping on his sister whilst she was taking a bath. He felt glad that he wasn't there. Brawls never solved anything. He finally chose to leave it alone.

Ishmael sighed softly. He had been ready to hold back Ash if he had somehow tried to aggress. If it had been him, he was definite he would have at least attempted a slap. Never and Ash glared at each other for a while. The emotional tension was high, but not applicable physically.

'And I guess you homo-liked your brother's ass as well. Is your mother interesting to watch when she is bathing, hey, Nev? I bet you peep a tom on her too,' Ash said in a pruned tone. The next thing he remembered was bone biting bone and he was down before he knew it.

'Fuck you!' Never menacingly glared down at him.

However, he didn't advance. Ash, coming about, held his aching jaw checking its status. His tongue flared – he had bitten himself in the process. He slowly got up and simply glared at Never.

Nothing? Ishmael and Winster were shocked. They were expecting to stop a fight here. After being landed a perfect cut on the jaw and being floored, Ash simply did nothing. *How can someone control himself like that?* Unless perhaps he knew, he wouldn't stand a chance.

'There, are you satisfied?' Ash said in a cold voice that would have scared a lion to back off. 'You have really waited too long, haven't you? Since my sister gave you the shoulder because I told her that you suck, you have always wanted to do that, but didn't have a good excuse doing so. I hope you aren't so mad. See, I know you very well now, Dotona. Diana doesn't give a shit about you, and Brenla no longer sees you as that *guy*. What more, Lotando doesn't give a damn about guys and that creeps you the pain. Yana – I won't even start, you'll double over. Suddenly no one sees you as the almighty Dotona Casanova. Three full weeks and no score, you have indeed sunk.'

Ever blazed with fury, Never pushed Ash as hard as he could. Ash reeled backwards towards the sleeping area and tripped over Ian's body. He fell with a groan. He looked up and saw Winster and Ishmael holding Never back from further aggressing.

The realization came upon Ash like thunder. He looked at Ian who was still peacefully sleeping. Surely, he had stepped over him. It wasn't possible that Ian had ignored it enjoying dreamland. With the havoc all around, Kheda must have woken up to see what was going on. Ash looked down at Ian near where he had fallen. He was smiling at him, but his face looked very pale – like sort of white.

He kneeled and shook Ian. 'Ian, hey, Ian!' *No answer.* Ash wheeled around and did the same with his twin brother. *No answer – what the hell!* He went to Kheda and shook him.

Kheda was solid rock. Ash's mind began to spin. He felt like a merry go round going round very fast not seeing anything at all. He forced himself to focus and placed his fingers on Tawanda's throat. *No!* He went over and did the same with the twins, and it was the same result. *Hell no!*

'Oh my God!' he screamed.

The others stood in their tracks and stared at him.

There was sniffling and shouting all over. The Torture Chamber was disorganized of chaos. Three occupied sleeping bags were at the centre.

'What the fuck is going on?' Never shouted pacing back and forth. He looked at the sleeping bags and his face transformed off colour. He paced faster.

'I must be dreaming, I must be dreaming,' Daniel was trying to collect himself, but it wasn't a possibility.

Derrick had Yana's head on his shoulder as her tears dripped and stained his shirt. She was sobbing horribly. 'What happened, Derrick?'

'Yeah, what happened?' Godfrey was anything, but cool and calm at this moment.

'My children, please, let us settle down,' Father Mango's face had horror and fear all over it. He was practically talking to himself. The ladies were naturally crying except for one who was perhaps too warped to even see.

'Settle down?' Pondai cried. 'Father, are you crazy? Settle down?' he gave a sarcastic laugh. 'We have got three dead bodies here and you bloody tell us to settle down?'

'Hey, Pondai, cool it!' The source was definitely Colodia, who was no longer crying, but her eyes were as red as cherry. Pondai glared at her for a while, grunted and said nothing.

'How did this happen, Derrick, can you please give us some freaky good answers for God's sake,' Ash blew at the medic who was trying hard to device a suitable reasonable answer. No matter what answer he was going to give, he knew it was useless. *Why the hell did I even agree to come? We were going back home today.*

God's timing is sometimes completely twisted. The unlikable source of thought came from Father Mango. *Why do these things happen and end this way? That girl surely had a point. Why?*

'Please, can we all give him a chance to explain what he knows? God deserves respect even through difficult times as this. Let us keep our faith strong.'

'Oh, don't give me that shit, Pastor,' Godfrey bellowed out. 'This isn't the bloody time.'

'Godfrey! Keep your useless mouth shut. Ian, Ignatius and Tawanda are... dead and there isn't a damn thing we can do to change that. Why won't all of you stop making such a row and get something going for once. You all make me sick,' Lot shouted.

The others glared at her speechless. Lotando buried her face into her hands and initially felt tears dripping from her eyes. She would give anything in the world to go back through time, tear those admittance papers in front of the Dean. A dominating silence followed for a few minutes before someone spoke.

'I checked the bodies,' Derrick offered, 'and from what I have discovered so far from their teeth, lips, gums, eye colour and a few other things, the cause of death was poisoning. I don't know what kind of substance they took.'

Stunned, they stared at him. *Poisoning? How could that be possible?* Obviously not food poisoning otherwise they would all be dead by now. They looked at the three bodies, covered from head to toe by the sleeping bags improvised as body bags.

'I tried to check their blood samples, but I don't know what happened to my medical kit. It has vanished and all my equipment was in it.'

'What did you say?' Father Rosina was shocked. He had perfectly heard him.

Derrick didn't reiterate. He knew perfectly. Father Mango's heart pounded, burning. He staggered to sit down on one of the benches. Father Rosina helped him down.

'Gama, what in the world of God is happening here?' Father Mango said.

The mid-afternoon sunshine shone on his aged face, but he felt weaker and colder. He gazed up at the sky. The sun was now overhead. It was about eleven or twelve. *Now where is Mr Legondo? He is two hours late.*

A few miles away at a hotel, Mr Legondo watched as the woman undressed. He instantly bulled up. For a week, he had been enjoying variety pleasure. His wife was nothing compared to this. How he had so missed the old times, and man would he miss them no more. As she seductively climbed onto the bed, he felt himself growing harder, harder, and groaned. Life was looking up.

CHAPTER TWENTY – SIX

A Swift's Departure

'I think it's now one o'clock – where is Mr Legondo and the other drivers?' Father Mango asked. He wished that he hadn't agreed to the fact of using the Harare's crew bus on the return. 'Weren't they supposed to be here at around nine?'

Father Rosina glanced at the bodies and felt a chill. They had been carefully moved into a dark corner to preserve them from the heat although the weather was cool. He looked at the youths. Some were comforting each other sitting on the benches and on the floor whilst some comforted themselves pacing about furiously.

'I have no idea where they are. Maybe he had a problem with the bus,' he said, looking at him.

Father Mango moaned. 'But the other drivers could have arrived by now, with the Jeeps. We have got ourselves one deranged situation here, Gama.'

'You could say that again,' Father Rosina replied weakly. 'I suppose they too are waiting for him for them to come. He is their indication that we are indeed leaving.'

Lotando sat with Daniel who cursed constantly. She hadn't even tried to calm him for she was a total wreck herself. The faces of the handsome Kheda and the funny twins calling her Lotto continuously played in her mind like forever. *I'm cold, Lot – are you cold, Lot? I'm...* Her mind was berserk. She couldn't believe that she would never hear their voices again, never again were they going to make her laugh.

The way she was feeling was multiple of what she had felt when Grandpa Urey had died. She wondered how Yana felt. *Why did they have to die? Why did they have to die so cruelly? Why the hell did they have to die at all?* She could make out Daniel's lips flashing rapidly as he gazed down with dark pained eyes, but she heard nothing, but echoes of sorrow.

Never was still pacing. By now, he could have walked a kilometre or so. He cheated a glance at Diana. She was over crying, glaring at the ground absent-mindedly. He knew how she felt. He tried nothing. He kept on pacing, accelerating by each thought.

Poisoning? Yana couldn't believe it. *What could possibly poison three people in one day and leave the rest? They all looked well yesterday before we went for bed.* She had first seen a dead body at her grandfather's body viewing ceremony. The amount she had seen had increased during her studies. Being or about to become a doctor, seeing a dead body wasn't a pleasant sight or feeling. One never felt the same again.

'As you all know, the Jeeps were supposed to be here early in the morning. Please, don't worry. They must be on their way. They must have experienced some problem with the bus or something. When they arrive, we'll have to go and bring the police here,' Father Rosina said, informing them on proceedings. It was apparent that he was talking to himself. He returned to sit with Father Mango.

Time passed and they estimated it as currently three in the afternoon. There was still no sign of Mr Legondo or any of the Jeep drivers. The youths began to get exceedingly restless. *What was really going on?*

'Where is the driver?' Brenla finally asked the question.

'I don't actually know what has happened to him, Ms Hewstone. Something must have definitely gone wrong with him or the bus. If there was any means of contacting him, we should have known by now,' Father Rosina sympathetically replied.

Lotando eyed him long, something in her memory suddenly nagging her. *What was it?* She couldn't remember.

'Wait!' Ash suddenly cried out. They all stared at him. 'I brought a cellphone along with my luggage just in case I needed to use it sometime.'

Without needing to be told to fetch it, he ran over to the compartment where their luggage still habituated. He was back in a flash. His face looked hopeful as he came over to join the group and held it out. It was a Samsung. He pressed the power button. *Nothing!* After a few seconds, sweat began to drip from his brow. Almost everyone had gathered around him waiting in true anticipation.

'What's wrong with it?' Lotando asked, glaring at the phone's touch screen.

'I don't know,' Tawanda replied, furiously depressing the power button. The screen remained murky, not responding to the stimulus.

'Dead battery I suppose,' Derrick alleged.

'That's not possible. I had it switched off before we left Harare and it's been off ever since. The battery was new. It couldn't wear off that fast,' Ash protested, floundering with the battery cover on the phone's back. It took a couple of seconds to prick it open. 'What the –?'

Everyone groaned. *There was no battery.*

'What's the idea of carrying a phone with no battery?' Never was offended. The hope had turned hopeless.

'I swear – I had a battery in there. I checked it twice before packing it,' Tawanda was too stunned.

Godfrey laughed mockingly. 'Then where is the battery, damnit! Someone took it, hey?'

Tawanda glared back at him. 'As a matter of fact, that's the only explanation.'

'Oh, bug off, man!' Never drifted away from the crew.

Everyone dispersed, including Father Rosina who hurried back to attend to Father Mango who was extra-worried by the fading hope. Lotando stood her ground and put a comforting arm over Ash.

'I swear it, Lot. This thing had a battery when we left home. Why would I carry it then leave the battery?' Tawanda was hysterical.

'I know, Tawanda, I know. Cool down and think about something else,' Lotando comforted.

In a matter of less than twelve hours, things suddenly began to make no sense at all. That's when she remembered it. *Father Rosina being given a phone by the Jeep driver.*

'I think we should go and look for some help,' Brenla offered. The audience projected their attention at her. 'It's still bright, we can reach the farm or the station where people rent transport into these woods before it gets dark.'

'How is that possible?' Never blustered. 'With all we have got, it's impractical.'

'We follow simple directions,' Brenla stood firm. 'We leave everything here and carry only what we will need along the way.'

'What about if the drivers happen to arrive whilst we are gone?' Winster asked doubtful.

'What about if they don't arrive?' Brenla countered. She was shaking and her hair was a total mess. It could have been representable if she had kept it braided before leaving the Chamber. 'We can't just stay here waiting for people we don't know are coming or not,' she added, gazing at the three bags in the corner. Her stomach churned.

'Yeah!' Never shouted. He was practically the most nervous of them all. His pacing mitigated nothing.

Whoever said boys didn't cry was wrong, Lotando thought staring at him. There were identifiable aftermaths of one who had been weeping.

'I think that's a good idea. Who knows, our driver might have hit a tree or maybe sick as we speak, or even… dead. We better get going,' Never said with confidence.

'Don't say such things, Mr Dotona. Mr Legondo is pretty safe. They all are,' Father Rosina offered. He glared at him apprehensible.

'What I am saying, Father, is a thought that may very well turn out to be true,' Never replied heatedly. 'With all due respect, Pastor Rosina, this isn't a fucken game.'

'Who ever said this was a fucken game, Mr Dotona?' Father Rosina shouted, losing his cool.

The tide was slowly turning. Three dead bodies were just too much. The Harare crew stared at their youthful Reverend stunned. This was the first time they had ever heard him swear or shout. Even priests are human, but anyway a lot of swearing was being spawned into the Chamber's atmosphere at the moment.

Never shrugged. 'What I'm saying is, if we don't do something soon, something is surely going to give. Look at it, our driver and the others with the Jeeps were supposed to be here by nine in the morning. What time is it now? I have a good guess that it's something around three. Perhaps the old man forgot all about us or has gotten himself into a tight spot. All we know for sure is that some of us didn't wake up and we have to do something very serious about it. We can't rot here and wait for someone whose whereabouts we don't know. If it reaches five o'clock, we are surely damned. It's obvious we won't sleep tonight until Ian, Ignatius and Tawanda,' he paused, pained. '... are somewhere safe. All we can at least do is to find the nearest help we can get. The more we are sedentary here, the more our minds will crack and one of us is surely going to freak out. If we make a move, that will keep us on something to worry about. Waiting here won't do us any good.'

The air was still for a moment. Everything was silent. *Situations like death surely make people smarter,* Lotando thought, *and desperate.*

Never had said the most sensible thing all day. His age, only a few years younger than Father Rosina, made the clergy look stupid. Time had been completely wasted on nothing.

Father Mango breathed lowly. 'So you suggest we do what, Mr Dotona?'

'I suggest we do as Brenla suggested. We try to get to the farm or the station and we have to make it fast. Since we have no idea where the farm is, I think the station will be a reasonable choice. I am going, who is with me?'

Every one of the youth was up on their feet. Nobody wanted to stick around playing *undertaker* to three dead bodies.

'I think it would be wise if you all go with Derrick whilst I remain behind with Father Mango. It would be faster if you don't go with us. I assume Father Mango won't be able to keep up with your pace. Just in case anything happens, Derrick will be with you. On the other hand, if Mr Legondo or the other drivers turn up whilst you are gone, we will follow,' Father Rosina emphasized, taking out a map from his bag. He gave it to Derrick. 'This is an updated map of the routes to and from the Torture Chamber. Please use it well. We can't afford to have you lost. It's getting dark soon.'

The ladies put on their jackets and sweaters, as the boys waited, practically scared to go to their compartment to fetch anything. The pre-evening's air had suddenly become very chilly. The wind blew strongly onto the vegetation, which was noisier than they ever remembered. Father Rosina handed them five torches, and path-trail chalk markers.

Lotando felt sorry for Father Mango. He looked very pale. His age was making a nuisance of itself. After all, the three they had suddenly lost had been his responsibility. She somehow knew how he felt. Father Rosina had opted for a moment of prayer before they left, but a few seethed individuals didn't want anything to do with it. As a result, no prayer was made.

CHAPTER TWENTY – SEVEN

Black Eve

The gale's force encircled the Chamber causing some micro bits of stone to disintegrate from the walls. The wind was probably inhibiting the initiation of the evening's rains. Father Mango was forever grateful it hadn't started raining – that was if it was going to. Rain would cause a major problem, especially a thunderstorm. His youths' corpses would be majorly affected by such an anomaly.

'Father?'

Father Mango looked up. Father Rosina was holding out a jacket to him.

'Take it, Father, you are shivering.'

'Thank you, Gama,' he forwarded kindly, 'but in times like these, I bid it God-willing to suffer and endure the pain like Jesus did on the cross.'

Father Rosina didn't push it. The old man had had enough for one day. His eyes looked sore, his skin withered and blood drained. There would be the explaining to do later. This trip had almost triumphed, and Father Mango had almost had a happy old age retirement. Father Rosina put the jacket by Father Mango's side on the bench.

'Just in case you change your mind,' he said softly. 'Can I get you some water?'

'That would be kind of you,' Father Mango accepted the offer.

Father Rosina went over to the drinking water containers stashed at one corner of the Chamber's main compartment. He took a tumbler from the dish's package boxes and opened the tap. Nothing came out. He opened the container. It was empty.

'Oh, no!'

'What's wrong?' Father Mango panicked from a distance.

'Nothing to worry about, Father,' Father Rosina assured quickly. 'There isn't any water left in our containers. Maybe the girls used it all up when they made tea yesterday evening. I'll just go over to the borehole, I'll be back in a sec,' Father Rosina walked out of the Chamber.

The wind's rush suddenly stopped. Father Mango looked around curiously. Initially, he took in the Torture Chamber's huge spectacular view in one glimpse. His attention however staked at one dark corner. The three bags lay there unruffled. He eternally wished that this was some kind of nightmare and he would somehow wake up and everything would be okay. He rubbed his shoulders and felt a warmth sprinkle all over his body. All the years he had come across many people, prayed for many diseased, those dead, those he knew and didn't, it had been natural then. He comforted the remaining relatives to be strong, reminding them that it was all the will of God. *Thou shalt take what thee made.* He wondered how that would sound to the parents of these deceased children he had helped *kill*. Moisture droplets fell swiftly onto his head. Father Mango wiped it off gazing skywards.

'Please, God, not now, please don't let it rain,' he begged in whispers. Suddenly, he felt a warm sensation on top of his head. He held it and shrugged. *My hair is weaning off, soon I'll bald.* He looked up. He couldn't see anything. It was as if fog had encompassed his eyes. A few seconds later, he didn't see anything at all.

The natural mountain's vegetation grew taller and bushy as they descended. Trees began to loom in numbers and the narrow road they were following became narrower. By late afternoon, the mountain slopes were usually versioned by early evening hard downpours, but since it hadn't rained for two days, the stones and soils were compact.

Derrick led the way followed by Never who frequently trot on his heels much to Derrick's frustration. The sun settled swiftly as if it had a purpose to do so. They walked, almost jogging downhill in a husky, hushed manner.

He will never know how much I liked him, Diana thought. Tears began to well up. She wiped them off. If only things were more different. If only her father hadn't raped her. If only her mother hadn't killed herself. Things could have been different. Women aged twenty-five usually had children, husbands and good jobs. She on the other hand had attended school up to the fourth form with due respect to the church and Father Mango. She was highly qualified as an Executive Secretary. Life at first had been better on her first job, but that was before her ex-boss had almost forced intercourse on her one late night. She had been unceremoniously fired and due to her ex-boss's reputable status and influence, nobody wanted her in their businesses. She had hated men with all her soul then. That was before she had met Tawanda at Father Mango's youth gatherings last year. Tawanda had almost the same life growth as she had except that daddy hadn't raped him.

Agreeing to this camp had almost cost her her new job – working as a till operator at a supermarket branch in Dangamvura, but, as usual, Father Mango had sorted that one pretty fast. She wondered how the twins' parents were going to react when they found out that she had played a big *role* in their death.

'Do you have any idea on how they were poisoned, Nana?'

Yana looked up to see who had asked. Colodia was looking at her expecting any answer. She had no idea. *I have no idea,* Yana thought. There was nothing she could think of that could have poisoned them because she hadn't had a good look at them like Derrick had. She knew Derrick knew something she didn't. Yana shook her head in response her throat too cramped to speak.

Colodia slumbered and looked away. She thought about Tawanda, the twins. It pained her so much that her pace faltered. They were so young, so handsome and so funny. Life was so cruel sometimes. It was more like hers, but if she hadn't done what she was currently regretting, she mused, Tawanda wouldn't have died.

'Please, keep up people!' Derrick shouted from a little way upfront.

'Are you okay, Lot?' the voice sounded concerned.

Lotando looked up expecting to see Yana. She blinked shortly stunned. 'I'm okay, Brenla, you?'

Brenla looked down. 'To tell the truth, I am not. I've never seen a dead person before.'

'Well, you have seen three!' Lotando didn't mean it to come out as harsh as it seemed. She picked up her pace. 'I'm sorry,' she apologized.

'Don't be. Be sorry for Ian, Ignatius and Tawanda. They will

never see anything again,' Brenla replied. 'I'm beginning to regret
I ever came here.'

'Me too,' Lotando subconsciously agreed. 'The memory will
stick forever.'

'Are you girls okay?'

The girls looked up. Ash strode towards them. His face was
bruised on the chin and lip. His hair was as untidy as it could ever
be.

'We aren't okay – normally,' Brenla assured. 'How is your sister?'

Ash shrugged helplessly. 'Definitely not okay,' he replied taking
a glimpse at Chenai who was walking with Winster upfront.

'What happened to you?' Lotando suddenly said noticing the
change on his face.

Ash tried to look away, but Brenla caught hold of his right
cheek and took a survey. He forcedly looked away, leaving Brenla
grasping the air, stunned.

'What happened to you, Tawa?' Brenla reinforced Lot's inquiry.

'Believe me,' Ash didn't look at her, 'you don't want to know.'

'Which lane do we take?' Derrick asked Never who stood next to
him.

The road took two labels, one on the right and the other on the
left going down like a V.

'Which do you think will be faster?' he asked pointing at the
map.

Never briefly measured the map with his eyes, and then looked
at both roads. He had no idea. The map didn't help either. The
roads were drawn in a skewed manner. He had another look at the
roads disappearing off into the woods.

Pondai arrived at their side. 'Why did you stop?'

'Look, we have got to choose between these two roads,' Never
explained. 'You are a civil engineer, right? Maybe you can do the
draw.'

Pondai looked at the map. He had experience with maps, as his
profession required, but the fact that he had been a sales executive
for the last two years made him lose his confidence. However, he
could tell that the map was badly illustrated. It was hard to tell
which was which on the map although they were named. A few
seconds later, all fifteen were gathered around Derrick trying to
figure out which was which

'There must be some sort of signs around pointing out, like sign posts, I mean,' Lotando offered.

'That may be true,' Derrick agreed. 'Let's look around.'

The search went on for a few minutes. Curses filled in the air.

'What's the idea of looking anyway,' Jack suddenly said. 'Both roads lead us to the station, let's just pick one and get on with it.'

'Aha!' Derrick suddenly cried. They looked at him. He was now standing in front of a huge tree. 'I found one.'

Ishmael could see a rusty metal plate nailed to the tree. The words written on it had long corroded, difficult to descript from a distance. He moved closer.

'It says...' Derrick wiped the smearing dirt off its surface.

Something snapped from the plate. A creaking noise suddenly pieced the air. He looked upwards and the object impelled directly into his forehead. The creaking was accompanied by another groaning noise whose source was unknown.

Ishmael felt the back of his head explode. His body flew air born and his stomach landed onto a hard jagged timber wood branch. Blood spewed instantly. Deafening screams pierced the air.

CHAPTER TWENTY – EIGHT

Dead Candy

'We have got to go back!'

'Stop shouting, bitch!' Never shouted back. 'Go back where?' His hands were smeared with crimson.

'Don't call me a bitch!' Yana flared.

She stepped up to him menacingly. Hitting someone would surely do her a lot of good and release lots of pressure. The tears in her eyes dropped, but she wasn't crying. That era was long gone. Lotando pulled Yana back from trying anything stupid against Never. This wasn't the day to mess around with anyone. At that moment in time, there was no telling what anyone would or wouldn't do.

'We aren't going back,' Godfrey announced. 'We have to continue – this is getting no better.'

'And what?' Yana cried at him as Lotando desperately tried to hold her back. 'And leave them here?'

'What do you want to do, Yana?' Godfrey spat back. 'Carry them? Face it – they are dead and that's just it. We are fucked up, but we have to move.'

'They will be eaten by wild animals if we leave them here, Godfrey,' Yana contested. The tears dropped some more. She knew they couldn't stop now, and that no wild animals existed in this region, the fiercely deadly ones that was.

Things had gone worse.

Brenla couldn't believe she was awake. It was like living a real nightmare. A log designed to be a spear with a medical surgery knife fitted upfront had killed Derrick. The knife had cleanly protruded into his skull as he had looked up, awkwardly going down to the throat where Yana had circumspectly removed it. Yana had been exposed to the world of surgery far too quickly and unwillingly and Derrick had been killed by one of his missing instruments.

Ishmael was also gone. His intestines had been splattered into various pieces and the back of his head was missing a sum of hair. Yana guessed that he had been unconscious from the log's conch before the branch had impelled his stomach open. The two fresh corpses had been meticulously placed on a clear surface covered by a few jackets. For most of them, the confusion in their minds had made them know death as a normal transaction, all paralyzed to feelings.

'Something is not right here,' Colodia shivered as they prepared to move making sure that the two bodies were fully covered.

'Oh, you hadn't figured out that one yet!' Ash replied reproachfully. He got a leering glare from Pondai. 'This is meticulous.'

'What do you mean *meticulous*?' Yana asked wiping blood from her hands with part of the cloth she had torn off from Derrick's shirt.

'Don't try to act as if you don't know what I mean, Yana,' Godfrey intervened. 'Derrick said his medical kit was missing this morning. And that knife suddenly comes out of nowhere to stamp itself onto a log creating an improvised spear. It impels his head, another log suddenly swings out of nowhere to smack Ishmael on the back of the head, and he falls directly into a bloody sharpened huge stick and loses his insides out. Don't you get the picture, Yana? Someone planned this. Someone killed Derrick and Ishmael.'

The moment Yana had seen the medical kit's knife she had feared this possibility. There was no other explanation. Derrick had been expertly murdered. Someone had killed Derrick and Ishmael and the scary question was *who?*

'Which road are we taking now?' Shamiso suddenly brought all of them back to Earth.

The sun was barely visible, its orange light lighting the horizon. It was getting dark and the idea that the two victims had been killed made it seem more like a horror scene. Killers adored the dark. The others instantly read her mind. They looked at the two roads. The chances of meeting someone or someone coming across them were extraordinarily negative. Nobody used these forests, especially not at that time of the day.

'We use this one. Derrick and Ishmael didn't die for nothing,' Lotando said choosing the route Derrick would have chosen, the route whose sign was stained by his last breath's blood. They chose that way. They walked briskly in silence.

'I'm sorry, Yana,' Brenla walked at Yana's side.

Yana was too white to feel any envy towards the girl. 'Thanks, Derrick was a great guy. I'd really want to know why somebody would want to kill him or Ishmael.'

'Why kill Derrick?' Lotando glided alongside them. The two ladies looked at her. 'Well, I think firstly Derrick and Ishmael were very unlucky. Those things could have happened to anyone who could have ignited them and they happened to be the unfortunate ones. I think the one who formulated this will be far happy because, because, well, to make sure that none of us survived when the time comes.'

'I don't get it,' Yana looked confused.

Brenla looked downwards. She knew what she tried not to know.

Lotando shrugged. 'Of course you do, Yana,' she said impatiently.

Yana had this sort of irritating attitude of claiming that she knew something whilst she didn't know anything at all. On the other hand, if she said she didn't know, it was like she was putting it wrongly. She knew.

'If another attack creeps up and, better, injures one of us. Derrick would have made a great difference, which may still be possible considering that you can replace him. The question we all must be asking ourselves first is, *"why is the killer killing at all?"'*

'And who it or they are,' Winster contributed from up front. He shook his head trying to wake up from the nightmare. 'What the fuck is going on?'

Never, who was leading the pack, suddenly stopped. 'Oh, shit!' he stamped his foot to the ground.

'What?' they all muttered. As it was now dark, the torches were being utilized.

'Did anyone take the map?' he asked hopefully.

The thirteen glared at him astound. *The Map!* It had fallen with its prior holder and was probably emblazoned with blood.

'So where the hell did you think you were going?' Daniel asked him furiously.

'And who the hell did you think you were following?' Never squared up to him. *I'm one stupid brick,* he chastised himself.

Colodia pushed them forward. 'We don't have time to waste on fights. There is no way we are going to get that map now – so let's move on. Oh, give me the torch, Never!' she said snatching the torch from him.

Never and Daniel recoiled and slowly began to continue along the lane which became darker as they went deeper.

'If someone is trying to kill us, what about Father Mango and Father Rosina back there?' Shamiso suddenly said after a lengthy silence. The crickets' tweets grew louder.

The question caught them by storm. *Were they still alive? Was the assaulter after them too? Did it know about them?* The two priests were pretty defenceless on their own, that was definite.

'Maybe the drivers arrived and took them to the police station,' Chenai tried to alternate.

'Maybe not,' Diana spoke for the first time. 'Maybe the driver is already dead, and the Reverends are dead too and we are the only ones left.'

'And worse,' Jack added, 'we don't know where the hell we are going.'

Like a blockbuster scary movie, the moon was full and white giving them extra light. They walked faster after avoiding more conversations, but it seemed liked they were walking on a treadmill.

'Where in the world is this place?' Never cried out impatiently, almost in tears. His voice echoed out into the night.

As if to answer him, something glistened on the surface at about a hundred meters from where they were. They stopped abruptly.

'What is that?'

No answer came. Uncertain, they moved slowly towards it.

'Ah!' Never suddenly exclaimed in a breaking tone. 'It's a stream.'

The pace increased from the sudden realization. The stream was about two meters in width. It flowed gracefully like a film of moving silver cutting the cross sectional area of the road into the night to an unknown destination.

'There!' Never shouted.

He was pointing far ahead, yards away. From the distance, the structure looked like an old edifice built out of firebrick. Dry maize stalks occupied much of the landscape. The maize field gave access to the farm from the forest. A few yards from the maize field, the farmhouse had its lights on, but no movements could be discerned from such a distance.

Never raced backwards, then dashed and leapt over the stream. Godfrey followed then Yana, Colodia, Pondai, Jack, Lotando, Shamiso, Winster, Daniel, Brenla, Chenai, Diana and lastly Ash. Instantaneously, they carried on. The path grew wider, leading to a cleared field that was adjacent to the maize field. Broad meter-height river stones flanked the path's shoulders, in various settings. Small trees mechanically distorted some.

Never felt a strange feeling brush him as they passed one of the stones. The hair on the back of his neck erected. He looked around and saw nothing. As they were about a hundred meters away from the maize field, his eyes picked up something. *Was that a newspaper?*

'Wait!' he called out to the others.

The others halted in their tracks and wheeled around inquiringly.

'What the hell!' Never's projected light shivered. 'This can't be.' He boldly took a step forward and picked it up. 'Isn't this the map Father Rosina gave us?' he said walking back to them.

It was and where they had last seen it and where it currently was, they didn't want to think.

Never smelt some strange odour and felt the tip of his fingers slippery behind the map. He used his teeth to grip the cylindrical handle of the torch and overturned the map. Both the map and the torch fell as he stepped backwards trembling in the dark.

'What is it?' Ash inquired, snatching Lotando's torch and focusing it on the map. 'What in –?'

We are all sinners

The map's rear was all white except for these four words. They were written in blood. It seemed like the writer had used a paintbrush to do his or her work because the lining and the clear-cut edges were clearly mastered despite those smeared by Never's fingerprints.

'*We are all sinners,*' Diana read it aloud, her voice crackling like a tremor. 'Where did you get this?'

'There,' Never informed, pointing at the place of origin. Torches shone the place. 'And what in the world is that, I didn't see that before.'

On the stone where he had taken the map was a heap of black cloth. Ash moved forward about to further investigate when…

'Don't!' Chenai stopped him. 'Use something to pick it up, er…' she looked around and finally stared at the trees, '… a stick perhaps.'

Ash glared at her for a moment and ultimately saw her reasoning. He snapped a dry branch from a nearby tree and stepped over, a safe distance away from the pile of black cloth. He used the end of the stick to plummet the cloth upwards.

'This looks like a cassock. Two cassocks in fact, look – two collars,' he noted.

'And two torn cassocks,' Lotando said. The cassocks were mercilessly ripped up into threads. 'Correct me if I am wrong, but isn't that Father Rosina's cassock?'

The alarm was raised. A cloud of fear overcast them in the full moonlight. More troubling, when they had left the two priests, they were wearing the same garments that lay disintegrated in front of them.

Ash lifted the cassocks a bit higher for a better view in the moon. Suddenly, something dropped to the ground from the ripped material. He shone the torch at it. His heart leapt into his mouth. He dropped the stick and the cassocks and staggered backwards, stepping on Brenla in the process.

'Ouch! Hey?' Brenla cried in pain. She gazed at him and saw red terror lamented on his face as he stared downwards. She looked down and saw it. Of course, she screamed.

'Oh my God, are those, are those…' Pondai muttered trying hard to catch his breath as the torches shone on them. 'Are those… ears?'

Two neatly sliced off human ears trickling with fresh blood lay on the ground. *Someone cut off the pastors' ears*, they all thought. The cassocks, the ears – it was too much to bear.

Never sped off in the direction of the farmhouse. The others screamed and sprinted off after him.

Ash was at the rear as they raced off towards the farmhouse. His lungs burned for oxygen, but he didn't dare reduce his pace. They were heading for the maize field and Never was far up ahead. Suddenly, he heard a swishing sound. He glanced back and saw it instantly. It looked like a shiny Frisbee. It actually took him microseconds to figure it out. He trotted aside losing his balance and felt a searing pain clean his arm. The sound of ripping material came with his cries of agony as the *thing* flew by him. He witnessed it continue on its path all the way. *No!*

'Shamiso!' he shouted in despair.

Sprinting a few meters ahead, Shamiso turned and saw it coming. It sliced her throat at the same time. She rolled over falling like a rag doll. The *thing* was knocked off course by the collision. It swerved into the nearby maize field and chopped off a few stalks before ultimately coming to a stop.

Ash witnessed all as he fell. The moment he hit the ground, he was back on his feet near death's impulse giving him supernatural ability. He stopped over her and knelt to the ground.

'Shamiso, Shamiso,' his eyes were filled with tears of grief and pain burned his soul.

She was gushing blood from her throat – her eyes filled with nothing, but raw terror. He tried his best to stop the blood, but lost that battle in seconds. She writhed a few times and ultimately slumped. She was gone. Her beautiful face was smeared with lines of her blood, her hair all over stained similarly. He looked ahead. The others hadn't heard the chaos. They had disappeared into the maize field. He could hear as they forced their way through the field taking off a few maize stalks along the way. He looked back at where the *UFO* had come from. It was clear. *Was the source still back there?* His palms and clothes continued to drench with Shamiso's blood. He began to cry uncontrollably putting Shamiso's head on his shoulders.

Godfrey ran over lots of things he saw not. He didn't know where he was going. He didn't care. He wasn't going to stick around and let an anonymous *psychopath* cut his ears off. The darkness of the inner area of the maize field made it impossible to see where he was advancing. Suddenly, he saw something in a flash. It came flat directly aimed at his face. *My God, is that a plate?*

It looked like one of the ceramic plates they had been using at the Torture Chamber. The plate hit him flat on the face. The impact, his pace and the plate's force, made him go legs up front, back, backwards like a person given a punch on the face. The ceramic plate exploded into pieces and sprayed all over the night, some of its pieces coloured in blood. Godfrey fell on top of many maize stalks, clearing a small partition of the field. As he landed, his hands went directly to his face. It was covered with his blood. Astoundingly, he didn't know why he didn't feel any pain.

He was okay, he mused relieved, as he sat up. He began to wipe his eyes from the blood. They were okay, *thankfully*. That plate could have popped at least one of them, he thought. His hands felt incalculable cuts of varied sizes of his facial skin, slowly and certainly, as he felt them, the pain suddenly reached its threshold.

'Where did that plate come from?' he cried to himself.

'Done with the dishes?'

Godfrey froze in complete fear. The fear was too much to swallow. He desperately wiped the blood smears from his eyes and looked at the source of the voice. The last thing he felt was the garden fork's teeth making their way through the cavity of his chest with alarming force.

Pondai pulled Colodia with him, pressing hard on the maize remains. All he could hear was the sound of feet striking the dry vegetation, and their heavy gasps for air. His dreadlocks were harvesting a lot of brown grains.

How can someone actually cut off someone's ears? He thought petrified, running faster. Those things were movie stuff, not known in this kind of country. *What kind of madness is this?* He could imagine the *slayer* cutting off the two priests ears striping them naked and tearing apart their cassocks. He ran faster.

Colodia wished Pondai could just let go of her arm. It was hurting badly as he pulled harder. She ran behind him, expecting to tread over something and fall at any moment. They were racing in a field of maize filled with an expanse of dry stalks in the dark. There was no telling where they were heading. They were just going. Her lungs begged for mercy as their volume was critically beyond the normal temperature and pressure. She felt like passing out at any moment.

Without warning, Pondai reeled over taking her hand with him. Pondai fell with a stuttering crunch, getting a few cuts from the dry grasses on the way down. For the trouble, Colodia tripped over him and fell bottoms up on top of him. They lay like that for a while, Colodia on top of Pondai in a standard intercourse position.

Colodia spat out a couple of stalk's leaves and pollen grains. Her lips tasted salty. She didn't know whose it was, but she knew it was blood. Three inches from Pondai's face, she pressed herself up.

'Are you okay?' she managed to utter.

'I'm fine, can we do it?' he grinned and winced in pain.

'Do what?' Colodia asked confused. She read his thoughts and groaned. 'Oh, you are horrible,' she said trying to get her body up pressing over Pondai's.

Pondai smiled weakly at her. She smiled weakly back, and then watched his smile fade unceremoniously. His face abruptly corresponded into a dark fear she had never witnessed on it before.

'What is it?' she whispered shivering.

Instantly, Pondai grabbed her shoulders and twisted himself off the ground revolving Colodia to the ground superseding her place as she superseded his, pressing her downwards. A shuttering crackling sound differentiated the air. It was the sound of a sharp impelling object compelling its way through the spinal cord.

'No!' she screamed. Her eyes bored into the eyes of the attacker and she knew the truth. The blood from Pondai's mouth streamed onto her face. Pondai had tried to save her life. Her world went black. The wind blew peacefully across the fields.

Mr Legondo stared at his old plastic digital watch and found himself grinning. Lady luck had given him variety these past few weeks. He wished he could stay there forever.

'Hi, *mudiwa*. I'm having so much fun. Are you going to be here long?' she asked flirting.

'I'm yours forever,' his mind was suddenly versatile in realization. 'Er – what day is it today, pumpkin?' he asked.

'Oh, you are forgetting it's Saturday, are you?' the woman smiled, playing with Legondo's toes.

Oh, shit! He thought conditionally ashamed. *We are supposed to be home by now.* He thought of the priests and the youths still waiting for him at the Torture Chamber.

What will they think of me? He temperately wondered how his wife would take this delay and perhaps fear that he had been involved in a terrible accident.

Well, he thought once more trying to tie up the sticky ends of his mind's translation. *I will make up an excuse early tomorrow morning – er, the bus broke down or something. Father Rosina and Father Mango will understand. I am sure the youths won't mind enjoying the place one last extra day.*

'What are you thinking about, love?' the woman tickled his barefoot.

'You, of course,' and they continued their business. He made sure his last day in the mountains would be as gratifying as ever.

CHAPTER TWENTY – NINE

Devil in a Sack

Never gazed at his young brother lying obsolete on the farmyard lawn. They had almost made it to the farm. Fortunately, the farm had no night watchdogs and he had wondered if there were people at the farm at all. Despite the chaos going on in the fields, the farmhouse with its lights on seemed peaceful in harmony. He had heard *death* screams and he was definite some were dying back there in the maize field. Someone was killing and now he knew whom *it* was. His body temperature was far below normal. If the killer didn't finish him, he was sure he was going to die of fear.

Never felt the pain on his back intensify. His face was flat on the ground pegged by what he thought was a huge steel rod of some sort, probably used in manufacturing security bars. The rod had perforated through his left shoulder blade, mainly intended to go through the side of his heart. It had only missed it going in a couple of inches into the ground. He had never imagined that the killer had so much strength to execute such a complex act. However, he couldn't get himself up. He could only strain his neck to look at Jack.

What would their parents say? What would the whole country say when they made the headlines after their corpses were found, if they were ever going to be found that was?

His mind played back earlier memories of how he had witnessed five of his own die. He remembered leading the others into the maize field. A few yards of running, he had been stunned, as he had come out at a cleared place near the middle of the field. The first things he saw were three arrow-like impelling steel rods shooting towards them. An improvised bow was fixed to a small rotten carrier tractor. On its back was a steel frame, rectangular – missing one length. It was wired by some kind of wire he hadn't had the time to distinguish, but he knew that these wires had been triggered to give in when someone coming from the same direction as they had come disturbed a concealed twine that was set lining the cleared area.

'Get down!' he had shouted, but to no avail. He had *killed* Daniel, Brenla and Diana.

He was positive of this because after hearing tearing screams of agony, he had risen and ran past the tractor for the farmhouse. The only ones who had followed him were Chenai and Jack. He had no idea what had happened to Ash, Colodia, the Ureys, Pondai and Godfrey, but considering the screams, his heart pained at the fact that they would all be dead, and that only he, his brother and Chenai were still going. He wished the farmer had a gun or a very suitable weapon.

Many had just died, and he wanted to live to tell the tale. Along the way, they had lost Chenai who must have fallen onto another path. After a minute or so, he had emerged from the maize field onto the farmhouse lawns. The terrain from the maize field to the farmhouse formed a small sloppy basin and he had rolled downwards and woken up at the bottom to continue his escape climbing hard. His brother, despite being fat and all, seemed to have attained mystical power as he had led the way to the other side of the basin. Then Jack had disappeared from view meaning that he had ascended to flat ground barely visible to the steep arm which Never was climbing in pain.

It had been a simple sickening *thud* – just that. No screams or anything. Any weird sounds made all sense to him that day. They all meant instant death. He climbed as hard as he could and finally as he emerged from the valley, he was lifted off the ground by an enormous force. Rolling over, he had seen the *killer*. His mind had almost shut down.

'You? You!' he had said. 'I can't believe it.'
'What is it that you can't believe?'
'But why?' he had stammered.
'You'll find out in hell.'
The killer had advanced at him striking him full on the chin with the steel rod that now pinned him down hard to the ground. He was hit onto the knee and crawled howling. He looked at a

distance and had seen his little brother lying there, blood oozing from his head. The killer's final action had stamped his body into the ground like a nailed poster onto a tree.

His mind shortly stuttered to reel all the occasions that had transpired during the camp. The debates, his endeavour against Diana, the twins and Kheda's mysterious deaths, then he thought of Derrick and Ishmael's deaths. He thought of the screams that had violated the field, the ears, the ripped cassocks, and finally the killer's face. His vision blurred and he went black without further pain.

CHAPTER THIRTY

Revelation Plateau

The Ureys stared at the dead farmer. His chest was blown off by his own shotgun. His wife lay on top of him drooping blood from the backside. Judging by their awkward positions, they had had time to protest. The picture wasn't a pretty sight to the three, but they had seen worse. Eight hours of death had made them numb to reason. They knew only fear and desperation of survival.

Lotando pinched her nose from the stench of faeces that soaked the floor. They were possibly released by the seizure of one or both corpses. She looked around. The room was silent. She and her two cousins had figured themselves unlucky at first when they had broken from the group in the maize field's disarray. They had heard numerous screams, agonizing death sounds and shouts of names, but they hadn't stopped. Like the others who had made it far, they had kept on fleeing from the unknown attacker.

The notion of reason, trying to figure out why they were being hunted was no longer an issue of concern. All they knew was that they wanted to survive and nothing else mattered. Winster had been the first to emerge from the maize field into a backyard. He had called out to the others who had followed his voice to the site. The light from the kitchen lit the backyard of the farmhouse. A station wagon occupied the ground closer to the door, which was uncharacteristically open. Anticipating safety, they had dashed inside only to find an old man grasping a shotgun and a woman lifeless, both dead. By the looks of it, they were dead for about an hour or so.

'We'll never leave this place alive,' Yana cried petrified. 'The killer has passed by here.'

Their only hope had been the farm at which they had expected to come across the assistance of the farmer or anyone. They had not only found the farmer, they had also found his wife and the two didn't look like they would be of any assistance.

'What shall we do?' Lotando said in commotion. She was cavorting all over the old-fashioned kitchen.

'We must find a phone or something,' Winster shook.

That was probably going to be their last hope for survival. They needed to call just anyone. He doubted that anyone was going to find *any one* of them still breathing, that was if they got hold of that anyone. The girls guessed his idea and began to scavenge for a telephone. They found it in the sitting room. The room was expanse. It prided itself with old-fashioned furniture, a fireplace glimmering with dying orange flames. A sofa facing the fireplace had water all over it.

Near one of the windows, at which they had seen one of the lights from the woods, was a small cabinet that had a landline telephone. The three looked at it from a distance. It was there, but who to call?

Dozen numeric answers splinted into their heads simultaneously making it practically difficult to think of one number. The front door leading directly into the sitting room from the farm's front yard suddenly burst open. They wheeled around, their hearts in their mouths.

When they saw *him*, they were somewhat surprised. A wave of relief encompassed them. That was before they saw what he had in his hand. It looked like a sword, despite it having bread knife teeth on its edges. They figured it to be some farm tool used for cutting rough raw materials like leather or small tree branches. They reserved the confusion and time to think for later.

They dispersed in all directions running for cover. Lotando felt her head being blown off by a heavy solid object. She reeled over and hit the shoulder of the kitchen door's access panel. She fell back into the sitting room in pain. Dizzy and unable to see a thing, she struggled to get up. She felt a punch on her nose and screamed in agony. Her face was filled with warm blood.

Winster saw him attack Lotando first and was indecisive on what to do. The shock and disbelief made his knees buckle as he desperately looked for an alternative. They were going to die and, guess who the killer was? It was incredibly crazy.

The killer raised the weapon aimed at Lotando. Yana reacted quickly. She grasped an empty decorating vas from a nearby cabinet and aimed for the killer's head. With all her might, she fired it at the killer and it hit the killer's shoulder. The killer staggered sideways and hit the walls. The killer grinned and looked back at Yana, a few meters away.

The killer grinned at her again. Yana couldn't believe it. It was like she was frozen, unable to move or run. The killer went for her. Yana's ability to feel her feet came almost too late. She managed to duck the blade by inches.

The second swing however caught her, slicing her t-shirt and grazing her shoulder's skin. The cut was deep enough to make her shout in sprinkles of pain. The other swing sliced a few strands of her hair and then back to the face, the boot connected perfectly. Yana felt her head slam to the wall. As she rebounded almost unconsciously, she pushed the killer away with all her remaining strength.

The killer lost balance and fell backwards.

Piece of cake, the killer thought. Suddenly a pain the killer knew not pricked the killer's nerves sky high. It came from the back. The next thing the killer heard was the sound of something like a nail being forced into a tyre. The killer's stomach's screamed and the sharp object emerged from the killer's abdomen clean with a few droplets of blood.

Lotando watched as the killer staggered to the walls holding the pointed sharp end of the fire poker that Winster had inserted through his back. The killer slammed to the wall, tried to pull the poker out from upfront. All, but the handle was stuck on the killer's back. The killer slowly fell, ended up sitting back against the wall, blinked and stared at them as Winster and Lotando helped Yana up. She was barely conscious. The killer's mouth began to drip with thick blood. The three Ureys watched in silence.

'You win,' the killer said, words gurgling blood.

'Why?' Lotando asked feebly. 'Please tell us why.'

'Like Mr Dotona said,' he said. 'This is no fucken game. You have a great insight about what life is all about, Ms Urey, but unfortunately that talent is wasted on technology.'

'Why kill all those people?' Winster asked, flushed.

'We are all sinners. We are all killers. Remember, Mr Urey, you killed me and this will haunt you all your life.'

Winster felt very uneasy. He had killed *the killer*, but if he hadn't done it, his cousins and he would have been it by now. 'Ian, Ignatius and Tawanda, that was you – wasn't it?'

Trying hard to sustain the pain from getting to him, the killer groaned. The fire poker protruded awkwardly from his stomach.

'I had it all planned all along and someone was kind enough to help. I had wished to start this major game of ours long back, but then your debates were more exciting, so I delayed. I thought of letting it end, and finally conclude it with a bang. I gave those three boys doses of cyanide during the night. Even Derrick knew that, but he was too afraid to say it aloud without knowing where it came from. And the boys slept like pigs, they didn't know anything when I did it.'

'But you are a man of God, Father Rosina, why do such devilish things?' Yana was filled with tears.

Father Rosina looked at her. 'Since God killed my family, I have been waiting for so long to repay him. I was only three short, Mr Urey wasn't kind enough to let me finish.'

'God killed your parents?' Winster quizzed.

'My father was a good man. My family died because they believed in the church, its stupid meanings, forgiveness bullshit was all indoctrinated in them. My mother forced me to attend services every Sunday, but I was never up to it. But then there was nothing I could do about it since my father was a great man in society. His position in life made me and my siblings follow the way of the church. We were expected to do good all the time, to lead by example. Oh, fuck that shit! With about ten years in service, my father, the greatest priest in our region, was going to become a Bishop. Many like him had been eyeing such a prestigious position for years. They all wanted it, but my father was the likely candidate to grab it. Things started to happen. It all became a controversial issue, controversy in the church. Some didn't like the idea of my father becoming the new Bishop because of his well-known ideologies of introducing changes. My father was tattooed by various attacks from several harassment schemes from financial fraud cases to sex scandals, but somehow all of them failed to bring him an inch down. The people of the Anglican Church believed in him. They wanted him to be the Bishop.

Two weeks before being given the title officially, I was at one of my friend's house at a party. I enjoyed it and stayed as long as eleven in the night. When I returned home, a crowd of people surrounding what had been our house met me. My ten-year-old sister, sixteen-year-old brother and my forty-seven-year-old father had been burned to ashes. Only my mother had somehow survived the explosion, but she was under intensive care being treated second-degree burns.

After that, someone got the Bishop's position and my mother never recovered. A month passed and she deteriorated daily. The main reason was that she refused to be given any medication, relief pain pills or anything to make her get better. She always told me that if she had to live, it was God's will. If she had to die, it was God's choosing. Yet, God had let people get along with murder. She was a coward. The case was never investigated because many people were bought to cover up the loose ends. My mother died the following month and all together, my family died because they believed in God. So you see – I repay God with what he paid me.'

The three glared at him astound. His voice had grown fainter as he talked. He was dying slowly. *How could someone so cleric be so insane?*

'But why did you become a priest?' Yana chocked out.

'To learn from the *master of death*. I thought I'd change along the way, burn away all the hatred, but it matured. I found joy in killing, being able to take souls and reserve souls. It was remarkable that I found my inborn talent at Parish College. I broke someone's neck for calling my dead mother names. He was never found. Along the way, I found pleasure, dealing with prostitutes, filthy rich men, miserable women and children who raped each other. They all cried for mercy before I paid God back his tokens. If put to hand, my record is exceptionally adorable,' Father Rosina swaged. His face was turning cold.

'You are sick,' Lotando snapped. She imagined all those people who had mysteriously disappeared in the papers. *Could they probably be the ones he was talking about?* 'You brought us here to play your sick game and add us to your body count?'

'Actually, that wasn't my idea,' Father Rosina eyes lit up in the dull light. 'Someone offered me someone special, in return for the rest. The person knew of my record from somewhere. It was a perfect deal. With Father Mango's nine and them six and the *special one*, I couldn't refuse the fun part of it. I was eager and since the person was the major funder of this trip, it was really kind.'

'What are you talking about?' Winster didn't know if the man was as mad as a cluster of psychopaths or what? 'What is this about the special one? You are truly cuckoo crazy.'

'She is special in a way.'

'She?' Winster gaped.

'Yes, she is. After all, she was smarter than all seventeen heads put together,' his voice was now hard to hear. The blood from his mouth had dried.

'Who is she?' Lotando asked feeling her nose hurt.

'You, of course.'

Lotando was confused. *The special one,* she thought very confused. *Why me be the special one? Special for what?* 'Why am I special?'

Father Rosina stared past them and grinned. 'You don't know shit, do you? Ask him.'

The three Ureys followed the intenseness of his gaze to the opened front door. They almost fainted as the gunshot echoed.

CHAPTER THIRTY – ONE

Siblings of Masscult

When she had seen Father Rosina holding that knife, her heart had almost stopped operating. It was beyond reasonable sense. Now she was paralyzed from her hair to the toes. Only one day, only one day had truly showed that the world was truly insane. She felt what her cousins felt. She knew it was much worse.

'Father?'

Lloyd Urey held a smoking *Manurhin MR-93* – a high-class sporting revolver – aimed at them. The last bullet had finally silenced Father Rosina. Father Rosina's head proclaimed a nice small hole on its focus. He had died knowing.

'Yana,' he grinned at them advancing inwards.

He kicked the door to shut behind him. The door's long frosted glass window rattled at the force, the door refusing to shut, leaving a small gap open. The pistol remained trained on them.

'What the fuck is this?' Yana shouted wobbling up. A bullet barely missed her shoulder. She fell down for cover.

'Stay where you are, all of you,' Mr Urey warned in a stern voice. 'I won't repeat that again and I am a good shot.'

What? Lotando couldn't breathe. Uncle Urey had almost killed Yana, his own daughter. *Was this the end of the world or something?* Whatever it was, it surely made no bloody sense.

'Father, you are the person Father Rosina was talking about?' Winster managed to breathe at last. His shocked blood ran all over his ears.

'Your father died long back, Winster,' Lloyd Urey said. 'It's a pity he never got to tell you the truth, dear brother.'

Dear brother? Now what was this? Lotando couldn't bear the pain in her mind as she tried to think.

'You mean you aren't my father?' Yana shouted, sitting up at a safer distance. 'And Grandpa was…'

'Yes, Yana, the man you called Grandpa was my father,' Lloyd Urey interjected. 'And your father. You are my step brother and sister and you were made to call me your dad for certain reasons.'

'What does that make me?' Lotando asked subconsciously.

'Oh, you the special one are the anomaly to all my problems. You are the mystery I never solved. Christine found you somewhere. I've spent the last decade trying to find out where. She always knew you were special, her diary said so much you wouldn't even dream off. You aren't like other people. Have you ever noticed that?' Lloyd pursued. Lotando blinked. 'The only people who knew about it were Christine, your foster mother. Yes, she wasn't your real mother. That secret died away with her and our father. Even as I heard, young Yana wanted to find out too.'

'Who told you that?' Yana was petrified. Only one person knew.

'Oh, Yana, dear sister, you thought this camp would somehow be able to make you know what our father told Lotando, as she was the last one to talk to him – she and that friend of hers? Mother told me about how you told her about your careful plan. Tell me, Yana, did Lot tell you anything you wanted to know?'

Yana felt a pang of guilt. She had found out completely nothing. Something her stepmother as now presumed – her grandmother then – had told her had made no sense. Grandpa Urey had promised to tell Lotando something just before he had died. They had been interrupted by a phone call, Debra's cellphone. That had been it.

Lotando glared at Yana. *So that's what this trip had been all about*, she thought, *Yana the investigator. Look where you put us now you piece of crap.* She looked up at Uncle Urey – she still couldn't believe it, but she knew it wasn't a dream. It was so real to feel. Twelve people were now dead, and that was reality. All killed by one maniac, unleashed by someone she had called uncle for the last nineteen years.

'You killed Grandpa Urey?'

Uncle Urey gestured the pistol, upwards as if he felt like tossing it away playfully. 'How can I kill my own father? Although he was still in the way of my beneficiary status, I couldn't kill my father.'

'So he was murdered after all,' Yana sighed. She felt a migraine coming hard and fast.

'People have their own problems. My dad wasn't one of mine.

Lotando and her mysterious place of origin were. I just played pong.'

Lotando fumed. 'Admit it! You killed him, someone saw you in the kitchen just before we left.'

Uncle Urey smiled. He pointed the pistol at her. 'So you figured that one out as well. Unfortunately, you are wrong. When your friend came back to collect her forgotten cellphone, father was indeed asleep, and I was looking for a beer in the fridge. He was an old man and, you know, with old age – swift naps.'

'Why did you pretend to be our father for all this time?' Winster began hands on laps. 'Who are our real father and mother?'

'Your father, as I said, was my father,' Uncle Urey shrugged. 'Your mother, I don't think you have ever met her. She goes by the name Tessa, Daddy's young mistress then. Father and I made a deal when you two were born. You were to be under me as your father so that mother wouldn't find out the truth. Your mother eventually didn't want the responsibility and unfortunately moved out of the country long back and she is said to have married someone. The plan worked marvellously and you have been calling me father ever since. Christine found out about this one dark secret one day and always refuted the idea, but she kept her mouth shut.'

'So what are you going to do to us?' Winster tried to keep calm.

'I'm sorry, but as I had planned, my brother and sister weren't to be harmed under any circumstances. Lotando was supposed to be tortured to reveal what my father and sister knew. He wasn't supposed to be this reckless, show his face. It didn't work that way, so I am really sorry that I have got to finish up the job Father Rosina started. I can't afford to have all of you alive as you know too much now. It's frustrating that this was all for nothing – Lot remains a mystery unsolvable it seems,' Lloyd Urey claimed backing away towards the door, carefully pointing the revolver at them. 'Time to die little ones.'

Yana managed to get up onto her feet. 'You won't get away with this.'

Lloyd laughed jeeringly. 'And who is going to stop me? Look at it this way, a lunatic clergy tried to have some fun and unfortunately died at the hands of you, the last ones to be killed by an anonymous fire. By the time anyone gets here, you will all be burnt to ashes. Nobody will ever find out. As your father, I get to inherit the fortune our father left you two.'

'I still don't understand,' Lotando tried to get up. Father Rosina's blows had been too severe. 'Who killed Grandpa Urey, if you didn't and why am I so special to get you to fund a camp trip for Father Rosina to kill people? That doesn't make sense at all.'

Lloyd Urey stood head back to the door watching their every movement. He didn't wish to end up as his accomplice sitting *death* on the floor. 'The last part of your question, I can't answer for this whole idea has gotten me nowhere in finding out anything about you that I don't know already. My sister and father covered their paths well on your secret. The other question, well, hell hath no fury like a woman scorned.'

Only Yana knew what that meant. Grandpa Urey had hidden his children's originality with his child. Someone must have found out and got very raged enough to kill him. She slumped. It had only taken eight hours to change life into a complete wreck.

'Now, who goes first?' Lloyd Urey pointed the gun at them.

The three stared at him petrified. They were all going to die after all – Father Mango, his youths, Father Rosina and his own youths. It was all going to be in the papers and the police minds. It was an end none had never envisaged possible. It was a tale many were going to read, retell and shudder over. It was a tale where all of them had died ugly deaths.

'I caused this. It would be fair to start with me,' Lotando stood forward for a perfect view for a shot.

Lloyd smiled at her. *Strong as ever to the end, maybe that's why you are special.*

Lotando stood shaking. *How had the others felt towards the shadows of their own deaths?* They would never know why they died. It was so sad. *I am going to be on the front page of the papers again,* she thought downcast. *And my friends, how are they going to feel?*

'No, I'll be first,' Winster staggered in front of Lotando.

Lotando tried to ward him off, but he suddenly had that near death strength. He stood like a true warrior.

'This whole idea of coming here was all mine,' Yana suddenly said. She came forward forcing a sob back. 'I was the one who persuaded you Win and forged Lotando's signature for us to come here, taking the bait Rosina had set for us. I'll be the first to go. After all, *we are all sinners.*'

'My pleasure, dear sister, see you in the afterlife,' Lloyd grinned at her and levelled the gun at her forehead.

Yana closed her eyes. She thought about all those they had come with. Ash, Brenla, Chenai, Jack, Never, Godfrey and her cousins. They were blown by the winds of insanity, their lives taken by the gods of ultimate evil. *At least I won't survive to remember all this.*

The sound that came next wasn't the one she had been waiting for. Shattering glass broke the air.

She screamed opening her eyes to see as steel rod impelling from Lloyd's throat. The door's window was no longer there. Lloyd choked, blood flowing from the edges of the hole created on his neck. The steel rod had penetrated through the voice box making Lloyd's chokes sound like gurgling water. The gun fell towards the ground, and he followed dead.

The door squeaked open and someone fell in, face front. His shoulder was pulsing awesome amounts of blood staining a white shirt into somewhat grossly maroon. Yana ran over and turned him over. She applied pressure on his wound.

'Never, Never!' she screamed.

Never saw her through fogged view. Her face was swelled up pretty bad. He had seen and heard the last bits of the *confession* from Mr Urey and, with the rod Father Rosina had pinned him to the ground with, he had gotten his revenge and possibly *saved* the Ureys. He was grateful that the front door had a window designed on it and that his aim had been perfect and just in time. He tasted salty liquid falling onto his lips like rain from the sky, Yana's tears. His vision at last went black.

CHAPTER THIRTY – TWO

Inadequate Perfusion

Four police escort cars raced along the road with a bus in the middle. The bus rolled smoothly along Ruwa's tarred road. The *driver* knew that his life was forever a mess. He knew that things could have been a whole lot different if he had only remembered one thing in his whole life and that was to have been *there* at nine in the morning. At least if he could have been killed, it would have been much acceptable. He would have possibly died a hero.

Thirteen people dead. It was all unbelievable. He knew that his life would never be the same. If his wife and children forsake him, he couldn't agree with them more. He had messed up pretty bad and he deserved even a knife to the heart to purge his soul.

Lotando felt the bandages on her face. They had gone to Mutare being eleven, excluding the bus driver. They were returning to Harare being eleven, excluding the bus driver including a senior police officer.

The numeric statistics hadn't changed for the bus, but gender and variety stats had. She felt everyone in the bus. At the back seat lay Never, his shoulder heavily bandaged. Nearby, Yana attended to him. They chatted in silent tones.

On the other seat sat Chenai with a sling over her left shoulder, bandage onto her forehead and a swollen lip. She had her head resting on Winster's shoulder. She seemed to be asleep. On the front seat, Daniel had his arm over Brenla's shoulder. Her injury wasn't bad, but it was effective. She was asleep.

Diana was asleep on the other seat behind Lotando, her head resting against her jacket. Her face was designed by numerous cuts and bulging bruises covered in bandages. She slept dreamless in peace.

Colodia was having nightmares, but a warm caring hand belonging to Ash kept her stable. His other hand was bandaged on the top.

Only Lotando and Diana sat alone and she knew she felt better that way. The dying was all over. The mourning had just begun.

...adjourn

www.ingramcontent.com/pod-product-compliance
Lightning Source LLC
Chambersburg PA
CBHW030301130626
46549CB00002B/646